Q Jayne

Praise for *The Cobu[...]*
Royal Plots and M[...]

'An important addition to Victorian stu[...]g book. Deploying new material from the Coburg archives, *The Coburg Conspiracy* illuminates the darker side of Prince Albert's impoverished and ambitious family... He also convincingly explores the evidence for and against Albert's illegitimacy.' – **Sarah Bradford**, bestselling author of *Diana and Elizabeth*

'A fascinating, riveting tale based on ground-breaking research.' – *Majesty* magazine

'Great detective work.' – Dr Christian Goeschel, Birkbeck College, University of London

Praise for *Retribution*

5.0 out of 5 stars What a ride!
Ashrae, an Amazon top 500 reviewer

'Mr Sotnick has the ability to explain in layman's terms all of the legal procedures, explaining them so well that, at the end of the book, I have new incites as to the workings of some aspects of the legal profession. Enough anyway to have enjoyed the ride this thriller gave me immensely…
All in all, a brilliant legal thriller.'

Anne Tanner, Amazon

Richard Sotnick's new book 'Retribution' is one of the most exciting, gripping and absorbing books I have read in a long while. He is definitely in the same calibre as John Grisham. It is one of those books you simply cannot put down. I eagerly await his next book. Read it !!

About Richard Sotnick

Richard Sotnick is a former Lord Mayor of Portsmouth and retired lawyer (Senior Partner of a Hampshire firm of solicitors).

He is a former chairman of the Portsmouth Cultural Festival and a director and trustee of the Mary Rose Trust. In 1985 he was elected an Honorary Alderman of Portsmouth.

His passion for music, and his role in founding what is now the Wigmore Hall London International String Quartet Competition, led to him being awarded the Walter Wilson Cobbett Gold Medal by the Company of Musicians. He also received honorary fellowships from The Guildhall School of Music and Drama and Portsmouth University.

Since his retirement Richard has devoted himself to his other passion, research and writing.

Richard's first book was *The Coburg Conspiracy: Royal Plots and Manoeuvres*, the story of how Queen Victoria's uncle worked behind the scenes to ensure the Coburgs dominated monarchies throughout Europe. Richard's passion for research led him to learn German so as to be able to read Court documents in the original. He unearthed unpublished letters from Prince Albert's mother that shed light on the prince's legitimacy.

His second book, *Retribution*, is a fast-paced thriller set in London's law courts, the Costa Blanca and the casinos of Las Vegas. In Richard's own words: 'I hold a mirror to England's judiciary; stipendiary and High Court judges. Although *Retribution* is a novel, lawyers who practised in the 1970s and 1980s might recognise some of the characters!'

Richard lives in North London with his wife, Ruth, with whom he has three daughters: Juliet, Lisa and Karen.

THE GODS DIVIDED

A Story of the Enduring Power of Love

'Many waters cannot quench love, neither can floods drown it.'
Song of Solomon 8.7

Richard Sotnick

Ephesus Publishing, London

First published in Great Britain in 2017 in paperback by
Ephesus Publishing

A CIP catalogue record for this book is available from the
British Library.

ISBN 978-0-9557125-5-5

Typeset by Geoff Fisher – geoff.fisher@yahoo.co.uk

This book is dedicated to the memory of the late Tony Snelling who was my inspirational English teacher at The Portsmouth Grammar School

CONTENTS

PREFACE

I was introduced to Olive Bell by Lawrence Bloom. Together with his cousin, Dennis Bloom, I travelled to Rieux-en-Cambresis in northern France for the Consecration of the Tombstone held on 27 May 1999 for Benjamin Bloom, who went missing following the crashing of his Lancaster Bomber in the early hours of 16 June 1944.

This is a unique story of love between Olive and Ben that endured for over fifty years. The doggedness, through veils of despair and family hardships sustained over this long period by Olive, who never forgot nor ever gave up her determination to find Ben and close the chapter on their lives, fills every page.

In many ways this is a tragic story of two people who found that religion stood in their way to a union of happiness and caused problems to their children. Religion forced them into a life of deceit with Ben's family.

I have a clear image of Olive, serene and dignified, understanding and forgiving, both in the cemetery at Rieux and at her ninetieth birthday celebrations in Suffolk at the Ufford Park Hotel on 19 April 2006. It was on that occasion when she asked me to write her story of her life with Ben and I promised her that I would.

My delay has been due to my commitment to my two earlier books and the necessary research into Olive and Ben's lives. I pondered for some months as to the structure of the book. This is not a biography and although I have endeavoured to keep to the accuracy of this remarkable tale, certain family conversations have been written for the tenor of the characters as they clearly would not have been recorded.

The Gods Divided has been a labour of love. I have found myself entwined in the lives of Ben and Olive and their families. It is as if I had been present as a silent witness to their movements and actions.

I hope that I have achieved in the presentation of this remarkable story a live and beautiful relationship which will endure.

Richard Sotnick
April 2017

Olive Bell, whom I first met at the cemetery in Rieux-en-Cambresis in Pas de Calais on 27 May 1999.

Pam Bell, who was devoted to her mother-in-law Olive, has given me memorabilia from the lives of both Ben and Olive, and has at all times given great encouragement.

My particular thanks go to Alan Bloom, who supported my decision to write and gave me his initial thoughts on the story.

Dr John Sweetman, who guided me through the maze of RAF research documents and stations.

Susanne Lumsden, my publisher, supporter and chief organiser in the production of this book.

Bill Ross "Operators Tale" – BBC post-war recording.

Rob Matthews and Judith Paskin, the editors.

Katherine Trail, who gave the final edge to the editing of the manuscript, and Julia Sandford-Cooke, the proofreader.

Emma Hardy, who designed the inside pages and Mina Bach, who designed the jacket.

Lynne Goldwyn, who advised on the history of the Bloom family.

Rabbi Steven Katz, who discussed with me the situation between Olive and Ben in the religious divide.

Simon Shulman of Graphical Agency for creating my website.

And to Ruth, my wife, for her continued support and wise advice throughout the years of research and writing.

PROLOGUE

Ben looked at his watch. It was 0120 hours on the morning of 16 June 1944. He calculated that they should be landing at RAF Waterbeach in Cambridgeshire at around 0250. First the debriefing, then, he anticipated with relish, the plate of egg and chips and hot tea, then a shower and a deep sleep until 1000 hours – always allowed following night ops.

He had only just become used to the continuous throb of the four Merlin Rolls Royce V12 petrol engines – which powered the Lancaster at some 250mph – when his new Lanc LL690J had arrived, with Bristol Hercules engines installed. Although noisier, they were just as stable. When he had asked why the LL609J wasn't good enough for the Rolls Royce engines, he was told they were making more Lancs than the production of Rolls engines could take.

One thing he he could not get used to was the sharp, pervading coldness. Despite his fleece-lined flying jacket and boots, Ben could not retain any feeling of warmth. It chilled his bones and numbed his fingers. At least it kept him alert and awake. It was worse in the winter at heights of twenty-five thousand feet. Now it was June, and they were flying deliberately low at just two thousand feet to minimise attacks from German night-fighters.

It had only been a few hours earlier, at 1830 hours, when the station commander, Wing Commander Wyatt, had entered the briefing hut to address the squadron on the target for the night. There were one hundred and sixty officers, NCOs and airmen seated on 'school chairs' behind rows of collapsible wooden tables. All sprang to attention on the order barked by the station warrant officer. When the wing commander and the squadron leader, Jimmy Jameson, reached the podium, the order was given to 'sit and attend'. The traditional no smoking during briefing sessions rule was complied with.

The wing commander came to the point immediately. He pulled the cord to unroll the huge map on the back wall, revealing the northern areas of France, Belgium, Holland and western Germany. He held a steel pointer, which he had extended to a metre, and placed the tip in the area of the Pas de Calais.

'Here, gentlemen, are your targets. You will bomb and destroy first the marshalling yards at Lens.' The pointer settled on the flagged town. 'When you have completed your bombing runs, and retaining half your bomb load, you will fly on to Valenciennes.' The pointer moved slowly across the surface of the map to the second flagged target.

'It is through these rail areas that the Germans are transporting troops and armaments to the Normandy beachheads.' As his pointer travelled across the map, he added, 'In all, there will be one hundred and eighty-four Lancasters, thirty Stirlings and ten Mosquitos – a total of two hundred and twenty-four planes in the attack on these two targets. These others will be taking off from RAF Marham.'

Ben's concentration deepened as the wing commander referred to his 514 Squadron.

'Visibility should be good. Little or no cloud cover and only light flak is expected. Avoid the airfields at Niergnies and Epinoy where the Germans have concentration of flak regiments.'

Ben could see Bob Hutt, the navigator in his Lancaster LL690J, making detailed notes. As wireless operator, he was relieved to hear the wing commander say there was to be no wireless traffic until the return journey, and then only if necessary. Internal communications were accepted since they could not be picked up by the Germans. He would be busy in any case, scanning for German night-fighter radio frequencies. Once located, he would tune one of the several jamming transmitters on board the aircraft to the frequency. This would stop the German ground controllers transmitting information to the night-fighter pilots. He could speak passable German, having learned Yiddish as a child from his parents.

His grandparents had arrived in England in 1897 as migrants fleeing anti-Semitic pogroms in Russia. They had arrived as most Jewish immigrants had come, with their battered old suitcase, very little money and no knowledge of English. The common language of the Jews in the shtetls of Russia, Poland, Lithuania and eastern Germany was Yiddish, a bastardised form of German and Polish which, over the centuries, had become the common language among their moving population. Ben returned his concentration to the briefing.

The wing commander concluded, 'Okay, guys, take-off will be at 2200 hours so all aboard and ready at 2145. I expect to see you all back here by 0300 latest for debriefing. Good luck to you all and beat the hell out of the Huns.'

Ben fingered the silver necklace given to him by his father for his bar mitzvah at the age of thirteen. 'This belonged to your great-great-grandfather in Lithuania. Wear it with pride and never take it off,' he had said to the young Ben. It contained the design of the 'Magen David' – the Shield of David – a Jewish emblem.

He joined the others on his flight in the sergeants' mess, where they ate their traditional meal of bacon, eggs, chips, peas, bread, margarine and jam, popularly referred to as 'plumar' because they couldn't tell whether it was plum or marmalade.

As usual, David Davis, the rear gunner, sat with Ben. He'd swap Ben's bacon for his eggs. 'It's always a pleasure sitting next to you, Bendy. I need your bacon and you can scoff my eggs. Here's to the Last Supper, guys.'

This was the traditional pre-ops toast. Like actors wishing each other 'break a leg' before the opening performance, it was a good luck comment ritually made on every occasion at the last meal before ops. The crew raised their mugs in token salute. 'To morning breakfast, everyone. Good hunting,' Joe Black, the engineer, responded.

Ben walked to his room and, as always, made sure it was tidy for his return. He hung his shirt in the cupboard, he replaced his towel by the shower and he left his letters from Olive in a neat pile on the table by his bed. He carefully checked that his writing pad and the fountain pen, which an uncle and aunt had given to him at his bar mitzvah, lay next to the letters. Once again, he touched his necklace. It was more than a lucky charm. For Ben, it was an act of faith – faith that he remained Jewish and that he would return safe and uninjured. This had worked for him on his previous ops. This was to be his forty-seventh.

Since his first flight over enemy territory in February 1942, he had been looking forward to his sixtieth, when he would be eligible for a week's leave and transfer if he wished. An operational tour for a bomber crew consisted of thirty non-aborted operational sorties. On completion of their tour, the crew would normally be broken up and rested by being assigned to various conversion or other non-operational units as instructors. It was not, however, uncommon for crew members to volunteer for a second bomber tour, and this indeed was what Ben had done. He had joined to hit the Hun and intended to carry on doing so while he could.

Bob Hutt had told him only yesterday that he was an arsehole for wearing his necklace on ops even though it was under his shirt, and if the station adjutant knew he would have forbidden it.

'Bendy, you really are a bloody fool. If you parachute out and get caught by the Nazis, once they see your Jewish badge, they'll probably shoot you. You're not giving yourself an even chance.'

'You may be right,' Ben had replied, 'but my father gave this to me on my bar mitzvah – what you would call your confirmation. He always wanted me to be faithful to my religion. In this way, I just feel I'm remembering him. It means something to me, Bob.'

'Okay, Bendy. Don't forget we've warned you.'

'Thanks, Bob, I'll take my chances.'

It was always immediately before take-off that Ben's stomach turned over. Eating, they had been told, was a major part of morale but, one hour before take-off, he did not feel that way. He was comforted only by the thought that experience had shown that, once the engines fired into life and the Lanc was rolling towards take-off, adrenalin kicked in and he'd be fine once again, concentrating on his job as wireless operator.

They were all there in their seats, waiting for the off. The Skip, Pilot Officer Ted Kingham, checked that everyone was at his station: Joe Black, flight engineer, seated next to Ted on a folding chair; Bob Hutt, navigator, immediately behind him, facing to the port of the aircraft, and then Ben facing forward beside Bob; Frank Spencer, bomb aimer, seated ready to operate the front gun turret; Fred Ansell, seated in the mid-upper turret gun; and David Davis, 'tail-end Charlie', the rear gunner.

Revving up the engines, Ted wished everyone 'Good hunting', his salute through the intercom to all on board – another comforting phrase which Ben, like everyone else, knew was the Skip's motivating comment as they began to move on to the tarmac for take-off.

The four engines screamed as the Skip opened the throttles to full and, before Ben could check the radio frequencies, they were airborne. They climbed to twelve thousand feet in formation of twenty-four Lancs. Other squadrons had earlier taken off from neighbouring stations, with other formations joining behind. This had been organised so entry to the bombing lanes over the targets would be staggered. The lead Lanc turned southwards towards Folkestone. They were to cross the Channel with the flight path between Calais and Boulogne close to Cap Gris-Nez, thereby avoiding the German coastal flak areas.

Keeping well south of St Omer, they joined the attack on the marshalling yards at Lens. By the time they had arrived, they could easily see the attack area lit up by explosions and fires with showers of tracer shells filling the sky. Ben was aware, as were his crew, that they could expect a more resilient defence from the German flak towers surrounding the more strategic areas.

Ben watched, mesmerised. How could they get through this seemingly impenetrable wall of fire? His experience cast away the terror of what he could see. He knew there was nothing he, nor indeed Ted, could do except fly the plane on its course and then get the hell out of the bombing lanes and on to Valenciennes. German night-fighters kept away from the target areas and left it to the array of searchlights and anti-aircraft batteries. Like prowling animals, the night-fighters attacked the bombers returning to their base.

Frank Spencer chose his spot as Ted Kingham brought him across the main rail junctions. As bomb aimer, Frank knew exactly when to release, and he could only part with half his considerable stock as they were moving on to Valenciennes.

Ben heard Frank shout through the intercom, 'Bombs away, Skip.' He noted the Lanc climbing to the right, away from the bombing lanes, and taking on the compass reading given by Bob Hutt.

Through the port side just below the wing, he could see one of the accompanying Stirlings had burst into flames. With half of its wing taken off, it was flying earthwards, out of control. He silently prayed the crew could bail out, but he hadn't seen any parachutes before it left his line of vision.

Before they had flown out of the bombing area, Ben had seen another plane in a downward spiral. This time it was a Lanc, though he did not recognise it as from his own squadron. LL690J had been lucky. They had taken no hits, and the searchlights had not caught them. Once one of the lights had caught a plane in its beam, other lights linked in so the bomber was caught in a web, making it an easier target for the flak guns.

Ben knew they could expect a greater concentration of flak at Valenciennes, a larger and more important rail centre than Lens. They would be there within twenty minutes. As they approached, they could hear the flak guns through the noise of the Bristol Hercules engines and saw the milliard of shells lighting up the sky in arcs from the ground. It was a frightening sight. The sky was lit up with thousands of coloured shells arcing up towards them. Surely this constant stream of fire must hit them. Ben's stomach muscles contracted and only the experience of so many operations saved him from kneejerk panic and loss of concentration. Once again, the marshalling yards were alight from explosions and fires from the mass of bombs showering down on the area.

Ted Kingham drew the Lanc on to the run in and let Frank guide him on to the target. 'Steady, Skip, steady. Nearly there.' The flak was increasing, and the Lanc shuddered from shells piercing through the fuselage.

'Bombs away!' shouted Frank through the intercom. The roar of the engines increased as Ted fully opened the throttles and lifted the plane upwards and out of the maelstrom of bombers on the path to the target area. The sky was lit from the searchlights and tracer shells pouring into their space. Ben could see below that the marshalling yards were chaotic with fires from developing explosions. Trains and goods carriages were thrown high into the air. The incessant blasts and deepening craters were creating a hell out of the rail centre. Ben saw three planes – two Lancs and another Stirling – crashing down to ground, bursting into flames. There was no time to ponder. The noise was deafening and LL690J was on its way home.

They picked up another Lanc, which stayed on its port side slightly behind. Ben heard Skip say he was coming down to two thousand feet to avoid, or at least lessen, the chances of being caught by a night-fighter. Ted was aware night-fighters generally avoided low altitudes. They'd find better pickings in higher areas.

Ben couldn't see the other Lanc but heard Bob mutter it

was joining them at that level and was too close for comfort. Ben's instinct was to contact the Lanc and tell them to steer off, but he wouldn't break radio silence until Skip told him to do so. He made himself ready.

He heard Bob tell Ted on the intercom, 'We'll be three miles north of Cambrai in three minutes.'

'Fine, too far from the flak area,' was the reply.

Less than a minute later, a shrill shout from Dave Davis alerted the crew to the presence of a night-fighter. Guns rattled from both the rear gunner and the mid-turret guns. 'He's firing at our neighbour!' rang out as the fighter swept over them and wheeled around for another attack.

'The Lanc's on fire!' shouted Dave. 'He's bloody close.' Ted took evasive action and they went into a dive onto their starboard side. It was to no avail. The Lanc on the port side had lost part of its wing in an explosion which had also taken out one of the engines. It was spiralling out of control. Its remaining three engines were screaming in a death throe, heard above the noise of Ben's Lanc. Its large fuselage came crashing into their LL690J with an incredible noise of steel grating and colliding with steel. A gaping hole appeared on their port side, close to the navigator's chair. Cold air rushed in like a gale, sweeping papers, pens and everything that was fixed to Ben's table out of the aircraft.

Ben, sitting just out of the area of the large gap in the fuselage and harnessed into his chair, remained in his seat. The moment froze into a strange paralysis with the noise of engines from both planes combined with fire and the crashing sounds of the adjacent plane breaking away. The wind suction was of enormous force, and Ben was horrified to see Bob swept literally out of the plane through the widening gap in the fuselage.

Ben heard, as did everyone else in the Lanc, the Skip say, 'We're going down. I'll do my best.'

The high pitch of the uncontrolled engines at full throttle after the transmission had been torn away signified the dying moments of the plane. The small town was fast approaching and Ted pulled hard on the control. This pulled the stricken aircraft momentarily upwards and to the starboard before it gave up the unequal struggle.

The plane missed the town of Iwuy by a matter of feet. Ben's last thought was how strange that, with the threat of imminent death, it was true that one's past life flashed across the mind. There was no time left. The crash came instantly.

1

July 1935

Frank Kimbell, the headmaster of Knapp Road School in Bow, in the heart of the East End of London, had sent a message for Ben Bloom to report to his study at afternoon break time. It was two days before term broke for the summer holidays. He was generally a kindly man who spoke softly and sincerely to his staff and pupils but, when disciplinary matters took over, he could be firm and cutting, both with his words and cane. He was respected rather than popular, and caps were raised politely when he passed his pupils in the playground or the streets. He'd acknowledge these with a flap of his academic gown or a hand raised from an arm with a bent elbow. He moved around the school in his distinctive firm walk, as if he had the most urgent appointment to attend.

'Ben,' he'd said, eyeing the fourteen-year-old boy who, although slightly short in stature for his years, exuded a happy and cheerful air. Mr Kimbell had always thought of him as a boy who had tried his best and was popular among his peers.

'I understand from your father that you'll be leaving us this term. Normally I'd have pressed for you to remain for at least another year. But it is common in this school for boys to leave at your age, and I understand your father is looking forward to you joining him in his factory in Hackney. Is this what you want?'

'Yes, sir. I need to start earning my living. My father wants me to learn shoe-making. I've enjoyed being here, though.'

Then, he added, 'Most of my friends in my class are also leaving at the end of term too,' as if this was his defence from being a disappointment to his headmaster.

'I understand. I can't stand in your way, nor would I wish to argue with your father. You have, however, obtained consistently good reports over your years here, and you would be a good influence on your younger brother. I think you would gain a great deal if you were to stay on and take your matriculation.'

'Well, sir, I have to do what my father says, and he's keen to get me to work in the factory.'

The headmaster sighed. 'Yes, yes, I suppose so but I see so many boys leave early when they could open their minds up to greater things. You have the ability to develop, and it's a bit of a waste. Any apprentice can learn to make shoes, but not everyone could move on to work which would stimulate your mind. You have a good mind, Ben, and I'm sorry you will not be making more use of it.'

He smiled wanly at Ben. How often during his career had he said similar words to leavers who had shown promise and could have gone on to greater things? He just hoped his pupils had learned to think for themselves. But he could not guide them against parental decisions, and in 1935, parents believed they had the right to determine their sons should follow them in what *they* were doing.

When Ben had announced at home one evening earlier in the term that he would like to become an accountant, his father had remained silent. His mother, however, had rounded on him. 'Ben, you'll go to the factory and learn to make shoes. What do you think your father has worked for all these years? It's to build up a business for you and Bob eventually to manage. You won't think of leaving him after all his hard work.'

Ben had recognised the moral blackmail that Jewish mothers, in particular, exercised against their son's independence from family life. If he thwarted his parents, it might sever relations to the extent that he'd be considered an ungrateful outcast who had brought shame to the family. There was, he knew, no answer. He was just sufficiently wise to realise this was an argument he could only win if he were to accept the consequences. At this moment in his life, he wasn't prepared to make such a family breach. He had stayed sullenly silent.

His school leaving report was excellent. 'Outstanding ability, above average. Top boy in class, regular and punctual, thoroughly reliable and trustworthy, willing and well mannered. A very intelligent boy with common sense and initiative' were the signed observations of his headmaster.

He'd been allowed one week's holiday after the term ended. He'd then been taken into the company's factory at Hackney, the signboard by the front doors proudly announcing 'Bloom & Phillips Co. Ltd', and introduced to the foreman, Joe Glass.

Joe Glass had been with the company for more than thirty years and had been foreman of the fifty staff for just over twelve years. He was now in his early fifties, although to Ben he looked much older. He was short at five foot four – similar in size to Ben, who was still growing. He walked with a rolling gait, and to Ben he seemed to have a permanent smile playing on his lips. The smile disappeared when he reprimanded staff for slackness or unacceptable behaviour on the shop floor. But he was respected and accepted. He wore a small *kippah*, a circular light-coloured cover for the crown of his head, in deference to his Jewish beliefs. Ben did not.

Joe took Ben around the factory floor, introducing him as the new apprentice. Most of the staff were women. They barely looked up from their concentration of cutting the leather to shape and the machines working on the shoes, but nevertheless made appropriate sounds of welcome.

'Good to see you', 'Good luck', 'Hope you'll enjoy the work here', 'Suppose you'll be our boss soon, so look good on us', were some of the comments offered on his round with Joe. Ben thanked them for their good wishes and was polite to them all. He did not question them as he knew nothing of what they were doing and didn't want to show his ignorance.

Joe explained the line of their work, from the large planes of leather to the finish. There was a pungent smell of untreated leather, made stronger by the odour of varnish and staining materials pervading the air, which was not unpleasant to Ben's sensibilities. Eventually, Joe came to the end of the sewing line and to the machines working to the finished product. These had to be examined individually for faults before they went to the packaging department. Here, three or four people were placing the finished shoes, each wrapped in light white tissue, into individual boxes.

Large white gummed labels with the style of shoe, size and colour in bold, neat writing were then placed on each box and transferred to the delivery room. Here, Ben saw hundreds of such boxes stacked up, ready to be dispatched to the retail shops or the wholesalers. Joe told him deliveries were made weekly, usually on Thursdays.

Joe also introduced him to the designers. Along with the foreman and directors, they wore white coats to distinguish them from the workforce, who wore their own informal clothes covered by the all-embracing apron. Finally, Joe took

Ben to the start of the process again to meet Shlomo, an abbreviation of the Hebraic name of Solomon. He'd lost a leg during the 1914–18 war, fighting in Belgium.

'Shlomo is one of our best cutters,' Joe said. 'He'll teach you how to cut the leather to shape as required by the designers. Here you start at the front end of the line.'

Ben took this to mean at the beginning of the process.

'We'll see how you get on. After a few months, I may send you up the line so that you'll learn to deal with the whole process. Then your father may send you out to meet the wholesalers and customers, most of whom are friends of your family. It's an old business, Ben, and many of our people were in this work back in the *heim* in the last century. Your grandparents and their parents were shoemakers in Lithuania, so it should all be in the family blood.' He laughed. 'You're a lucky boy to have such a rich inheritance.'

Ben donned his apron, which tied around his neck and his lower back, and sat with Shlomo. The older man took a sheet of leather and, without measurements, deftly cut the outline of a shoe, left and right. He then stretched the leather, cut it with a sharp blade and made it into the shape he required. Only after the fifth time did Ben venture to ask Shlomo if he could try. It took him several attempts before he obtained the right shape, and even then Shlomo would not pass it on for further work.

'Don't worry,' Shlomo said softly. 'It comes with experience. Within the week, I assure you, you'll be able to get the right lines. Here's a leather sheet. Practise on this.'

At home that evening, Ben's father Louis, who had always been known as Kivi and who didn't make a custom of speaking formally to his family, stood at the head of the table with his wife Caroline and the five children.

'Ben, Bob, Lily, Florrie and Kitty, this is a very proud day for me, your mother and the family.'

Ben could see that his father was struggling to control his emotions. His breath caught on the last word and he paused to breathe out slowly before continuing.

'My grandfather and two generations before him created a factory in the small town of Memel in Lithuania over a hundred years ago to make shoes of quality. They worked long hours, and they prospered. Their shoes were sold in the three Baltic States and further afield.

'Today, Ben has joined the family business. Ben,' he said, turning to him, 'this is a day to remember in our family's history as the torch begins to be passed on to the next generation of Blooms. Your mother and I wanted you – and Bob also when he is old enough– to take the name of Bloom & Phillips to greater heights. Always bear in mind, Ben, that 'quality' is our watchword, and I expect you to follow this word everywhere.

'The company has moved on since its inception as Bloom & Phillips, and you will take it further. When you have learned the trade of making shoes, you will learn the skills of business: the purchasing of quality leather, the recognition of marketable designs, the need to seek more efficient and cost-saving machinery, and the management of, and kindliness to, our staff, which is the most important of all lessons you can learn. Your understanding of financial discipline, banking and negotiations . . . Ben, you have much to learn, but you have begun today.

'There will come a time when you will be running the factory. I have every confidence that you will learn your trade and will be able to act with confidence for its future.'

At that, Kivi reached for the decanter in front of him and

poured out two shots of malt whisky. The girls were not offered – his mother didn't drink alcohol and Bob was considered too young. Kivi drank a toast to Ben, the latest employee of the company. Ben acknowledged the toast by quaffing his whisky in one long gulp.

Caroline, her hair cut short, underlining the severity of her looks and the tautness in her face, maintained her disciplined hardness. There were times, too infrequent for Ben, when she relaxed and found humour in conversation. Then a smile, not broad but a smile nevertheless, however thin, would appear. Ben could see – but not remember – that in her younger and more carefree days, his mother had been able to hold court among her contemporaries. But age and family responsibilities had taken their toll and an embitterment had begun to reach her soul. But tonight, Caroline celebrated with Kivi. This was a family occasion to enjoy.

She began to serve the soup and, as she did so, she added her pride in the evening's celebration.

'We've waited a long time for you to start working in your father's factory, Ben. Now you really *are* in the business. Wait till you can visit Uncle Morry and your cousins in Leeds. You'll be selling stock to them.'

Of course, Morry was not an uncle. All his father's close friends were addressed by Ben and his siblings as uncle and their wives as aunt. Ben, having been brought up with this part of his family's culture, felt comfortable with it.

He was not political but was intensely loyal: loyal to his friends and loyal to his religion. This may have surprised many who knew him well, because he was by no means a devout Jew. He attended synagogue on Saturdays because his father expected him to accompany him, and it was more a note of filial duty than of religious concern. However, at school, whenever he found anti-Semitism or unjustified criticism of Jews or their traditions, he defended them fiercely – with his fists when required.

A few weeks later, Ben found himself at home one evening with his parents and friends from their early days in London, Harry and Rose Steinberg. He was fascinated listening to their reminiscences and the severe hardships they had had to encounter: the struggle to earn enough to make ends meet at the end of the week, and the necessity to learn to read, write and speak English. Ben sat and listened. He did not join in the conversation or offer his opinions. He was the mute audience, listening to the players on the stage talking of a past world; a world he would never know.

Eventually conversation moved on to current times as he heard his father say, 'Harry, I don't know how all this is going to end. Look at what they say in the *Daily Express*.'

Kivi thumbed the pages until he turned to page eight, with its screaming headline quoting from Hitler's speech against the Jews in Germany and to his references to the recently passed Nuremberg racial laws.

'He's making the most frightful speeches against the Jews, Communists and everyone who isn't a Nazi. Here in England, who would have believed with all our history of democracy and tolerance that British fascists wearing Nazi uniforms of black shirts and jackboots – and led by a former Labour minister, no less – could ape this lunatic and have such a following? They're actually now called "Mosleyites" in the papers. Well, at least in the *Daily Express*.'

'Kivi, democracy means tolerance. Despite their opinions, these fascists are seen to have the right to express them. That is why the police protect their marches.'

'But look at them, Harry! They're nothing but a bunch of hooligans garnered from ex-convicts. They're ready to beat up people who oppose them, just like the Nazi thugs in Germany we read about. They have sticks and whips and claim using them is justified defence. The police protect them. They say it's their duty. It's a disgrace. They should be protecting us, Harry!' In his anger and passion, Kivi pointed his index finger at Harry as if to strengthen his point. His staring eyes and his quivering mouth could not conceal the genuine anger and contempt he held for fascists – in whatever country they did their work.

'Maybe,' Harry said, 'but we all know that if you dress people in black uniforms and give them authority, they adopt fascist attitudes. The police, after all, are the prefects of society. *These* are the ingredients of fascism.'

'You're right. This is *our* danger. The time will come in the East End when we Jews and the left-wing workers in the docks will have to defend ourselves. But it will be against the police and not the fascists, because the police will be protecting *them* in the name of democracy, not us. They'll say they have the right of free speech and free movement. It's not a happy thought. We – Jews, that is – are not looking for a problem, but the fascists will provoke us and use the police as their front guards. You wait and see, Harry.

'Except for the commies, no one is standing up to the Nazis, nor standing up for us, and nobody in authority is seeing what is happening to this country. Stanley Baldwin and his government are idle, and the entire nation is sleepwalking into an abyss. We were better off under Ramsay MacDonald.'

Kivi finished his whisky and refilled the glasses. Ben remained silent. This was a discussion between old friends, and he was aware that his contribution to the discussion was not welcome. He knew that when the time came, he'd be the one to fight – not his father nor Harry, who were too old for such actions. But he'd welcome it.

He was fifteen years old when the call came. He first heard it at the factory. Shlomo whispered in his ear, 'Have you heard the fascists are going to march through the East End? Through Cable Street, I hear. There'll be a real battle there. We won't let them through. It's an absolute insult. They'll break windows and arms and legs where they can. We won't be alone. The dockies, the left-wingers, the commies will be there. There's thousands of 'em. There's no way that bastard Mosley will get his army through. This'll be our stand.'

'Where can I help?' asked Ben. 'Who should I speak with? I want to play my part. We're all involved.'

'Phil Piratin is the leader of the defence league. He's not one of us. He's a commie, but he'll tell yer.' Shlomo paused. 'On the other hand, he's too important for the likes of you, and too busy. Have a word with Chaim Mintz. Tell 'im I told you to speak to 'im. You call at his house. I'll give you the address before you leave tonight. Don't tell yer father, though. He may not approve'.

2

21 September 1936

Ben took the number 56 bus by himself to Cable Street and, with his usual self-assurance, knocked on the door of Chaim Mintz.

A tall sturdy man, with a square-shaped head leading from wide shoulders and little appearance of a neck, opened the door. His short-cut white hair gave him the ominous powerful presence of a man you would not want to offend. Ben placed him as mid-forties.

'Mr Mintz, I want to help in the fight against the Mosleyites. Shlomo from my father's shoe factory in Hackney told me to mention his name. I'm Ben Bloom.'

Chaim looked at the slightly built figure in front of him. He saw the eagerness in Ben's eyes, and the determination in his face. They needed everyone who wanted to help. With volunteers such as Ben, he could muster several thousand. Being untrained, though, they'd have to be instructed as to where they should be and what was expected of them.

Chaim had fought at the Somme in the Great War. He'd been a staff sergeant, so knew what was required in training and discipline on the field of battle.

He'd been chosen by the committee to liaise with Piratin and the leaders of the Independent Labour Party to assemble a cohesive – and disciplined – defence force. It had become clear that Cable Street was to be the place where, in the words of Maréchal Pétain, 'they will not pass'.

'You must be Kivi Bloom's son. You'd better come in for a few minutes.'

Once inside the terraced house, Ben was taken into the front room – or the parlour, as it was called. Chaim did not offer any hospitality, nor did Ben expect anything from this important man. Nor did Chaim offer him a chair. He hadn't been expecting Ben and this was not going to be a long discussion. He would just hear the boy out.

'So, you're Ben,' he said.

Ben nodded, surprised he was already known.

'Does your father know you're here?'

'No, but he'll support me. I have to fight against the Mosleyites.'

'You might be too young and too small for the fight. We're dealing with experienced and hardened thugs here. If they smash in your head, they wouldn't care but your family might!'

Ben looked him straight in the eye. 'I can't agree. I'm Jewish. I fight my cause as you do. I can act as a runner or a messenger. I can throw weapons at them. I can pour oil and whatever down on them from the upstairs windows. There nothing I can't do to fight!'

Chaim surveyed the boy. *He's got guts. His mind is in the right place. Who was he*, he thought, *to deny this boy – not so much a boy but a young man – his right to do his duty as he saw it?*

He paused for a moment. 'The problem is that we may not just be fighting against the Mosleyites. It will probably be the police in their hundreds, trying to make a pathway for the fascists. It's called democracy, to enable the right of movement and the right of free opinion and speech to those who would deny these freedoms to us and many others. You'll be a great help, but only if your father agrees. Come to a meeting at the elementary school next Thursday. It's at the corner of Christian Street. There'll be a great number of our people there. Make sure you speak to me before the meeting and bring with you at least one hundred marbles. Collect them in tins from boys in your area. Tell them they'll be making a great contribution to our cause.'

He noticed the look of astonishment and disbelief on Ben's face.

'Ben,' Chaim said quietly, 'the police will mainly be on horseback. So, in these narrow streets, marbles will stop them forcing their passage. Horses cannot deal with marbles under their hooves.

'Thanks for coming to see me. I appreciate that, and give my warmest regards to your parents.' He ushered Ben towards the front door, and Ben had just enough time to thank him before the door silently closed behind him.

***

Ben picked up his friend Jack Curtis, who lived in the next street. They had both been at Knapp Road School and Jack was now working in his family's joinery business. The families had known each other before Ben was born. They still played cards twice a week in each other's homes, occasionally *klobiosh*, a form of rummy played by their parents in Lithuania.

Ben excitedly reported his visit to Chaim Mintz. He spoke quickly – at times too quickly – and Jack had to wave his hand at him to slow him down.

'Jack, the guy is massive! He fought at the Somme. He knows how to fight in a battle. He has so many volunteers and there are many more from the dockies and commies. It's going to be historic. There's been nothing like this in England. But Chaim is certain of one thing: Mosley will *not* pass through Cable Street!'

'God, you were brave even to knock at his door. He's got the reputation of being the great leader of the Jewish people around here. But I don't think my father would allow me to go, Ben. He wouldn't want me to get my head cut open, and I don't think I want that either. Why not leave it to the dockies and the commies? Why should we get into scrapes with the police? If you've definitely made your mind up on going, though, I'll help you with the marbles. My little brother, Mike, has a hoard, and his friends have plenty. They're always on the streets playing with them. Trouble is, they may want something for them in return. They don't have your enthusiasm to fight the police.

'Sure, I can give them a couple of bob for tins of two hundred. That'll be enough for a few ice creams and Fry's chocolate bars.'

'Okay, let's go and find Mike and you can talk your way into his bargain.'

It took the whole of Ben's week's pay but he got more than one thousand two hundred marbles from Mike and his friends and put them all into one large used paint tin with a handle, which Jack had given to him. He knew his parents would find out what he was up to and rather than face their anger because he had been too secretive, Ben decided to tell them his plans.

'Dad, I've met with Chaim Mintz,' he announced the following evening at supper. 'He said I could act as his runner between him and his commanders during the fighting around Cable Street, where the Mosleyites will be coming. He was keen to look after me, Dad, and he sent you his best wishes. He's a great man! He wants me to go to a meeting at the school in Christian Street on Thursday.'

His mother's voice thick with anger, she shouted, 'You're too young and you're not to get involved at your age with street fighting, particularly with the police! Quite apart from any personal danger, you could be sent to an approved school if you're arrested. What will that do for your future in this country? What respectable family would want a son-in-law with a criminal record?'

Her face was creased and her eyes rolled large with confusion, tears and, Ben thought, desperation. As she spoke, she waved her arms in anger as if to emphasise to her husband her strong objections.

Ben had witnessed his mother becoming emotional on many an occasion. He knew this could turn into an ugly hysterical rant with floods of tears so he appealed to his father; he knew his intentions would receive at least sympathetic support there.

'Dad, if I can't support what I believe in, where's my future? What will I *ever* believe in?'

Kivi looked at the fierce determination in the eyes of his son. He was quietly proud that Ben held such strong views and was so passionate. Had Kivi been younger and more physically fit, he would have felt and acted in similar manner. Despite Caroline's pleas, he could not deny his son's fervour.

Careful not to be too supportive, and also not to undermine the authority of his wife, he was, nevertheless, impressed with Ben's initiative in his meeting with Chaim, a man he wholly respected.

'Ben, you can go to the meeting at Christian Street, but you are to tell Chaim he has to look after you and not allow you to be in the front of the fighting. Tell him that your father, Kivi Bloom, explicitly told you to say that. I'll allow you to participate on that condition. Caroline, I'm sure Chaim will look after him and, if I know you, Ben, you won't let yourself get entangled with the police.'

'No, Dad. I'll keep my head down. I think Mr Mintz will only use me as a runner.'

'That's what I want to hear. Keep me fully informed as to what is said.'

On Thursday evening, Ben was surprised to find so many people walking into the school in Christian Street. He arrived a good fifteen minutes early and saw the crowds of people, mostly men, walking in files of seven or eight, as they did at football matches at Highbury when occasionally he went with friends to see Arsenal play.

The meeting started ten minutes late, probably, Ben thought, to allow the throng of people to push their way into the hall. The large assembly room was already packed. Many were standing at the back and along the side. A number, forced to stand outside when the stewards would not allow any more to enter the hall, were just about able to hear what was being said within.

There were no preliminaries. Chaim Mintz stood as chairman of the meeting behind a lectern which came up to the level of his stomach. He held no notes. He had no papers to place in front of him. Six of his senior aides and commanders stood on each side but a little behind him. Chaim was clearly the leader, the chairman and the spokesman for the meeting.

Ben noticed how Chaim waited and looked around the assembly room, raised a hand in a half salute in acknowledgement of the cheers of support, and then waited again. It seemed longer to Ben, but it was probably less than half a minute before there was complete silence and an aura of expectancy, with everyone craning forward in eager anticipation to listen to Chaim's words.

It was masterly. Ben never was to forget this experience;

a lesson on how to command and how to bring an excited – and rather undisciplined and noisy – throng of people to heel merely by invoking silence. By his dignified presence, Chaim created an aura of the importance of his message.

Chaim started slowly. 'We all know why we're here. It's all going to happen next Sunday, the fourth of October. Mosley's British Union of Fascists has thrown down the gauntlet to march through the streets of the East End to show their power and influence. It will end, Mosley has stated, with his usual party speech. He wants to show the Jews in particular, but also the people of this area and the left-wingers, whom he hates just as much as he hates us, that they cannot stand up to the might of the fascists.

'We all know what's going on in Germany. Mosley and his cohorts are simply aping Hitler and the fascist movement in Italy under Mussolini, both in their uniforms and their actions. If the Mosleyites win this battle, for this *is* what it will be, we Jews in particular can expect far worse things to happen in the future. They *must* not succeed. They *will* not succeed. We are *not* alone. There will be thousands from the Left with us under the leadership of Phil Piratin. We have liaised, and it is agreed that we shall stop any movement through Cable Street and adjacent streets. I want to meet the commanders after this meeting. And I want the commanders to tell you all the time and exact locations and to whom you should report.

'Wear rough clothes – clothes that you won't want to wear again. They may become torn, blood-stained and unwearable. So not your wedding suits.'

There was a ripple of laughter at the thought of East Enders in smart suits ready for battle.

Chaim continued, 'Come with defensive personal

weapons but no firearms or knives. We don't want it to appear in the press or on radio that it was the Jews who killed or maimed anybody. We are purely defensive and will protect our own.'

Here, there were cheers of support, and Chaim had to wait and raise his hand a number of times before he could continue.

'We need old furniture and heavy bric-a-brac of old mattresses, cushions and wooden poles to barricade the streets, sandbags and hosepipes which can be fitted to domestic water supplies, pillows with tarred feathers and other useful and heavier items which can be thrown from the top floors and rooftops. Please tell your commanders what you will bring after this meeting. We will then co-ordinate our defences.

'Commander Philip Game of the Metropolitan Police has spoken with Phil and me. He doesn't want trouble on the streets and has told us it's his duty to ensure the Mosleyites can get fair passage through the East End. It is, as he put it, their *right* to exercise freedom of movement along the streets of London and for free speech. I won't say exactly how we replied …'

At this, there was much laughter and raucous shouting. When Chaim calmed them down again, he merely added that the dockies, communists and the Jews had a right to defend their homes and a right of protection against the fascists.

'I told him that our elected representatives, the Board of Deputies of British Jews, has denounced the march as anti-Semitic. But the commander knew this and added that "the board had also advised the Jews to stay away".'

Here, there was much derisive shouting and laughter.

'What does the bloody board know of us in the East End?' shouted Max Follett from near the back of the hall.

Another replied, 'As much as the back end of my old horse!' to greater laughter.

Ben realised that members of Board of Deputies, which represented British Jews and was elected by the independent communities across the country, were out of touch with the strong feelings of the people who elected them, particularly the Jewish community in the East End of London.

'So,' said Chaim as he came to the end of his speech, 'we shall be defending ourselves not just against the Mosleyites, but also against their protectors – the Metropolitan Police. They'll come at us on horseback, supported with batons and shields with an army of police infantry behind.

'It may well be bloody, but we must not fear. These are *our* streets. They are narrow. There will be barricades. We expect injuries, and we have doctors and nurses on call who have volunteered their services.

'We must try not to be taken by the police. They're bound to prosecute. But just in case, we've appointed our own lawyers who'll represent us in court, as may be, without cost. So go to your street commander for more detailed instructions for Sunday. We've given you a map marked with their names.

'Good luck, everyone. We stand together and will defend our rights. We shall not allow what is happening in Nazi Germany to happen in the streets of London. Thank you all for coming and for your support.'

There were cheers and everyone began singing the HaTikva, the Jewish anthem.

Ben found it all very emotional. The passion of Chaim's speech, the strong united unwavering support in the assembly and the strength and loyalty behind their cause brought him close to tears. He felt as one with the people, and he knew that they were all at one with each other. He had never been to such a public meeting, and he wondered what more he could do to support.

Ben, who had been told only to be close to Chaim on Sunday, went to the front of the hall. Chaim saw him and beckoned him over. After finishing his discussion with a young and positive-looking man, he turned to Ben again. 'I knew you would come. Did you get the marbles?'

'Yes, many more than a thousand, nearer to sixteen hundred. I'll bring them on Sunday.'

'Good lad. Then stay with me. Come to 54 Cable Street at 2.30 p.m. on Sunday. I'll give you instructions. You'll have to keep close to me. I'll need you to take messages to the commanders and for them to inform you of their progress. You'll then report back to me.

'As for the marbles, they'll be handed to our men at the front end of Cable Street. In the meantime, acquaint yourself with the streets around here. Check the names of the commanders and the streets they are in charge of. Walk these streets forward and backwards before Sunday. I want you to know them blindfold.

'With all the noise, the clattering of hooves and chaos of the day, you *must* know where you are and where you're going at all times. Ensure you recognise each commander and know their names.' He looked Ben hard in the eye. 'Tell them your name and that you'll see them on Sunday during the battle. It's important that they also know you and that you're my runner. See you, Ben, on Sunday. On time, please.'

And with a wave, Ben was dismissed and Chaim turned towards another person waiting for him.

3

Sunday, 4 October, 1936

Ben arrived at Cable Street at exactly twenty minutes past two. He certainly wasn't going to be late. The whole area was buzzing. It seemed that at least a thousand people were milling around – mainly men but there were a number of women wearing headscarves.

The autumnal afternoon was still warm from the late summer heat. There had been no rain for some days. Old furniture had been moved into the street, and Ben noticed the same in Christian Street and the adjoining streets. Mattresses, old, shabby, stained and torn, were being stacked up across the streets at distances of some fifty yards. Old chair legs were in abundance behind the barricade and set against the walls of the terraced houses to be used, Ben realised, as clubs for self-defence.

Ben looked up and saw women leaning out of the windows, shouting above the noise across the street and to their next-door neighbours. From the meeting at the school, he was aware objects and a variety of liquids from questionable sources were being made ready for pouring onto the 'invaders'.

He walked through the open door of number 54 and passed a group of people in the narrow hall waiting there, all seemingly talking at the same time. It was, he thought, the dialogue of the deaf. No one was listening; everyone was talking. It was a hubbub of noise, shouting, chatter and general excitement, which made Ben aware that this afternoon was to be a historic occasion. He found Chaim in the front parlour with his agent and several of his commanders.

'Good to see you, Ben,' Chaim said. 'Come and be seen. Gentlemen, you all should have already met Ben, my runner. He'll be reporting to your posts from time to time. Give him the information he asks for and listen to my instructions through him. Take a good look, because there'll be no time for recognition when he arrives.'

Ben handed Chaim the two large containers holding the marbles, and Chaim passed these on to Paul Slotsky, whom Ben had met earlier that week. 'Paul, you'll know how to use these. You're in the vanguard and will be the first to meet with the police cavalry.'

'Thanks, Ben, these will be very useful, very useful indeed,' Paul said, with purpose in his voice.

'Right, gentlemen, let's get to our posts! Good luck. Don't get caught, and avoid injuries. We must carry the day. Ben, you keep close to me. I don't want to have to shout for you. And don't get involved with the fighting. We've enough troops.' And with that, he swept out of the room. People made a passage for him to leave the house, with Ben following in his trail.

***

Chaim stood with his agents and supporters by the first barricade, which was now some eight feet tall and spread right across the street. The withdrawal to the second barricade fifty yards behind was to be through the doors of three of the closest terraced houses, across the back gardens and then back to the street behind the second barricade. There was no gap in any of the barricades. They were too high and too wide for the horses to jump over.

Right on three o'clock, with military precision, came the police whistles and orders given by the police commander over a microphone to march forward.

It was later reported that there were six thousand police, behind whom were between four to five thousand blackshirts waiting in the side streets to the rear of the police. It was judged that more than sixty thousand anti-fascist demonstrators faced them.

As the mounted police began their march forward at a slow, steady pace, the uniformed police at the rear broadcast a message on the large megaphone.

'Attention, attention! We require right of passage. You are not to obstruct our officers in the performance of their duty. Any such obstruction will be a criminal offence. Arrests will be made. Prosecutions will follow.'

A barrage of jeers, boos and expletives met this statement.

Through another megaphone, this time from the Cable Street side, another message could be clearly heard over the noise. 'We'll never let the fascists through. These are our streets. Not yours. Not theirs. Fuck Mosley and his blackshirts!'

The chant of 'they will not pass' rose from the ranks of the defenders of Cable Street.

Ben could see the hordes of uniformed police astride their horses, some eight abreast. They were armed with batons, which they were wielding aggressively. Strong visors guarded their faces. They were a formidable sight. Behind them were the 'infantry' of scores of uniforms, marching in close order across the street, many deep, all wielding long wooden truncheons in a menacing manner, which could do great damage to head, face, shoulders or legs.

The police loudspeakers were continuing their warnings,

and the defenders were howling abuse and screaming that the fascists would never be allowed to come through their street.

It was at that point Ben saw the horses break ranks and rear up out of control. A number of riders, suddenly unable to control their steeds, were thrown from their saddles. Mayhem ensued, and the horses were panicking too much to take instructions. The defenders stayed where they were but watched as the horses plunged out of control, bucking and rearing. Ben stood and watched as the marbles – *his* marbles – did their work.

The first attack having been blunted, the police infantry came towards the barricades, wielding their long truncheons. But they were met head-on by hundreds of defenders before they had reached the first barricade. Screams, blood, shouts, profanities filled the air – and from both sides. Desperate police officers dragged their wounded from the frontline, and some of the Jewish fighters were grabbed and arrested. Other wounded fighters were taken into homes to be washed down, bandaged and given a cup of hot tea.

Chaim turned to Ben, who was now at his elbow. 'Get to Mark Levitsky, quick as you can, and tell him to send the next batch immediately to the second barricade. The first barricade is lost. Go, go now!'

Ben shot off and within two minutes and through gulps of air and heavy panting, he passed on his message.

'Tell him I'm coming with two hundred men,' was the reply.

Ben ran back to Chaim, who was already marshalling the defences to the second barricade. On his way back, Ben could see police on top of the first barricade and jumping down from it. But they were being drenched from the odious waters being dropped on them from the houses. Over the noise and chaos, Ben could see the police snarling and shaking their fists at the women who were emptying their Jerry pots over them. Over the din of the battle, he could hear their cries. 'You fucking whores, you bloody bitches, we'll get you!' they screamed.

Levitsky's men surged in from the Christian Street crossing and joined the fray in front of the second barricade. The fighting was now manic. No quarter was given by either side. Clubs, cudgels and chair legs were wielded with heavy hands, with no thought of what injuries they would inflict. Screams and loud swearing pervaded the air. Megaphones from both sides added to the noise and confusion. Blood was everywhere: on the street, on the pavements and on the clothes of the injured being carried off the streets of battle. Ben could see men being dragged away into houses with blood cascading from their heads. Others lay unconscious, having been hit by the long-handled truncheons of the police.

Ben, standing just at Chaim's elbow behind the second barricade, heard him shouting above the din, giving orders to shore up gaps in the barricade. He could see what was happening on the other side – police cracking men's arms, elbows and knees causing them to collapse in screaming pain. However, he could also see that the police were not getting everything their own way. They were dragging back several their colleagues, who appeared to be unconscious and covered in blood.

It was a scene out of hell, he thought. Most of the defenders who had been too injured to fight on had been taken into homes for safety and 'repairs', but the fighting was still furious. Via their megaphones, the police were threatening all sorts of retribution unless they were given free access.

The extra men from Levitsky had made a difference, and the police were now defending themselves between the first and second barricade.

It was 5.15 p.m. when Ben looked at his watch. He could not believe time had gone so quickly. The orders through the police megaphone continued. But then it seemed that the police in the front line were retreating towards the gaps they had made in the first barricade.

There was suddenly a lull in the fighting. Two policemen with white armbands and no weapons came forward to the front of the second barricade, the phalanx of the attacking police having fallen back some twenty yards. Chaim went forward to meet them.

When he returned after only three minutes or so, Ben overheard him tell two of his colleagues that he had been called with Phil Piratin to meet with Police Commander Philip Game further back along Cable Street. They had been given free passage to do so. In the meantime, it had been agreed that there would be no more fighting. Some twenty minutes later, Chaim returned and called out to his men that the fighting was over.

The police commander had told Mosley it would not be possible for his men to get through Cable Street and that the Metropolitan Police were pulling out to prevent more casualties. He had warned Chaim and Piratin that those the police had taken into custody would be prosecuted but that they would not be pursuing anyone else.

There were tumultuous cheers as the word was passed along. Many of the Jews had sustained injuries, some of them serious. The doctors and nurses were using the front and back rooms of the terraced houses in Cable Street as medical stations. Cries rang out all along the street.

'Bring in another crate of bandages!'

'More spirits here!'

'This leg needs immediate attention and cleaning.'

'We're putting this arm in a sling, don't try to use it.'

'You're in shock. Here are painkillers. Don't take any more tonight. And drink this hot cup of tea the nurse has brought you.'

Ben heard it all as he made his way through several houses to check with Chaim as to whether he was further required.

'No, Ben, the day's done. The day is ours! Thanks, and well done. Go home and tell your dad. He should be proud of you.'

Instructions were passed along to clear the barricades and put Cable Street, Dock Street and Christian Street back into acceptable condition. Already, smashed windowpanes were being replaced and broken doors refitted. Within days, no one would know that there had ever been a major battle there.

Mosley's blackshirts marched off to Hyde Park, where they held a rally and were addressed by Mosley and two of his henchmen. They were not followed by the anti-fascists and were left to get on with their retreat. So far as the communists and Jews were concerned, they had won. Cable and Christian Streets and the neighbouring area had, for the first time, stopped the blackshirts. It was a message to the rest of the country that the Nazi tactics of intimidation and violence in Germany would not work in Britain.

Later that year, the government passed The Public Order Act forbidding the wearing of uniforms or pseudo-military dress at public meetings. It was the end of organised fascist violence in Britain.

Many of the arrested demonstrators were harshly treated by the police. Most were charged with the minor offence of obstructing police and fined five pounds – a week's wages. But eight of the ringleaders were charged and found guilty of affray. They were sentenced to three months' hard labour.

Ben returned home without telling his parents the details of what had gone on.

'We won, Dad! After three hours of fighting, the police withdrew and told Mosley his blackshirts could not march through Cable Street.'

Kivi could see that Ben was not injured, and he didn't question him further after Ben had mentioned he had stuck to Chaim all afternoon.

But the newspapers the following morning were full of the reports and vivid pictures. It immediately became known as the Battle of Cable Street. The communists under Phil Piratin gave full vent to their feelings, and radical leaflets were passed into every home in the area. Communist supporters stuck placards to walls, claiming victory over the fascists. Phil Piratin became the local hero, and the following year he became the first communist to be elected to Stepney Borough Council. Later, in the 1945 General Election, he was elected as the communist candidate for Mile End.

The communists and dockers were portrayed in the press as the fighters, not the Jews, who had borne the major part of the battle. Ben thought it was a travesty of accurate reporting, but he acknowledged – from what he had heard – that Phil Piratin was a politician and streetwise in dealing with the press. Chaim had been content in victory; he wasn't in it for the publicity or adulation which followed. Nevertheless, Ben felt aggrieved at what he considered was misreporting of the facts.

Around one hundred and seventy-five people other than the police were reported as having received serious injuries.

That excluded the many more lesser injured who were treated on the day by the volunteer medics in the homes set up for that purpose.

Although Ben did not speak of his experiences to his friends or neighbours, word went round in his community. When he entered the factory on the following Monday morning, the women on the working benches looked up when he entered and gave him a long cheer and there was much clapping. Ben, embarrassed, blushed and moved quickly to his bench next to Shlomo.

'There you are, young Ben. You're an 'ero!'

'Well, I didn't do much. I was with Chaim Mintz all the time.'

'You were there, Ben. You were there. That's what counts.'

4

May 1938

In 1938 and in early 1939, two major events changed Ben's life.

Following the Cable Street battle, Ben had worked hard to assimilate the knowledge of manufacturing, design and marketing of high-value ladies' shoes. He had passed through all the channels of the factory, including distribution. His father had introduced him to the wholesalers and many of the shop retailers whom they traded with. He knew, of course, the 'wider family' in Leeds and Manchester with whom his father substantially traded. He now wore the white coat of an executive.

It was on that evening of 15 May 1938, that Caroline had organised a family celebration dinner at home. Kivi and she had invited their closest friends, Harry and Rose Steinberg, and Ben was pleased to learn that Frank and Jane Zedelsky from Leeds were also joining them. Frank was large in shoe retail in Leeds and, with the Zedelskys being so close to Kivi, they were considered part of the family. Ben had met them on his business travels with his father.

The evening was full of laugher and convivial conversation rose from the table. It was a noisy, excitable and memorable evening. Kivi had brought out his best vintage wines, kept specially for moments like these, and Caroline had prepared a large turkey. 'No good serving chicken or capons. We always have that on Fridays. It has to be different for a celebration, and I needed something large enough for us all,' she had said to the assembled company.

Caroline had indeed prepared a banquet. At least, Ben considered it a banquet. Frank insisted in giving a toast to the new director of Bloom & Phillips Ltd. 'I have no doubt, nor have we all in Leeds – and dare I say in Manchester – that in due course, Ben, you'll take the company to new heights.'

Kivi, full of emotion and hardly able to keep the tremor out of his voice, his eyes misty with half-concealed tears, spoke of his pride that Ben had become his co-director. 'It will be a great father-and-son partnership, even though we call ourselves directors in a limited company,' he said, with a twinkle in his eye and a laugh. 'I'm happy to have Ben's support. Caroline wants me to take life more easily but I must warn you, Ben, I have it in mind to go on for a long, long time!'

Ben grinned back at his father and laughter and applause erupted from around the table. 'Speech, speech!' they chorused.

'Okay, okay,' Ben laughed nervously. Public speaking was not something he'd done before, and he had not prepared anything.

'Well, well . . .' He stammered and paused.

'Come on, Ben, say something!' his mother said cajolingly.

'Thank you, Mum, for this wonderful dinner. I know it took you a great deal of time and we've all enjoyed it,' he said, to claps and shouts of 'hear hear' all round.

'I just want to thank Mum and Dad for all the encouragement they've given me. I hope I can help Dad and take a bit of the burden he's carried for all of us in this house over the years. I just hope I can measure up to your high standards and values, Dad. I'll certainly try.'

Ben sat down to loud clapping and shouts of 'Well said!'

***

The following February, his father had a heart attack in the factory. He was taken by ambulance to the city hospital but did not survive the night. He had been suffering for well over a year from pains in his chest, which could only be treated with pills that were palliative at best. They had, however, given him some relief when he had pushed himself more than he was able. Ben and the family – and Kivi himself – were fully aware of his medical problems. He had walked with a much slower gait for several months. He had had to stop every fifty yards or so to ease the pain in his chest which came when he exerted himself, even mildly. Caroline and Ben's elder sisters – Lily, Florrie and Kitty – had urged him to retire from work, and although he had confidence that Ben could now manage the factory, he had refused to give in.

'What shall I do at home? Just wait till I die? I shall go the factory as usual. I'm not stressed by my work, but I shall be if I don't know what's going on!' he would say.

Even though they'd all known Kivi was unwell, the heart attack had come as a great shock, and the family were distraught. Neighbours and friends called to offer their condolences, particularly during the seven days of shiva which Jewish people kept following the death of a close relative. They did not go to work or socialise but remained at home for visitors and the morning, afternoon and evening prayers.

Ben considered his position. His younger brother, Bob, had not been pushed to go into the factory nor had he had any wish to do so. He had left school and had struck out on his own, entering the insurance business as a junior clerk. His sisters were not expected to work in the factory and had made good their shorthand and typing training in London. They all had secure jobs as secretaries in offices in the city.

Ben knew everything depended on him now. He *had* to

run the factory successfully. He'd leave the day-to-day management with Joe while he focussed on expanding the business. He was fully aware that the family – and certainly his mother – now depended upon him. He immediately made arrangements to visit the family connections in Leeds and Manchester who were large in the retail of women's shoes.

In the two days since his return to the factory, Ben had been busy on the phone. He had confirmed visits to the Zedelsky family, where the three brothers ran an empire of over fifty shoe outlets in the Leeds area, and then on to Manchester, where he had arranged to meet with the Syssen family, who were even more powerful in the retail side. It was not the first time he had visited these families. His father had taken him with him on the last occasion some six months before, and he had received a warm welcome. They had known his father for decades, but this was business and nothing was ever given away. Since he had been a small boy, he had always been told that, when the families had arrived in England in 1896 from the pogroms in Lithuania, they had all agreed that Kivi and Caroline would work in London and build up a shoe-manufacturing business there. They would make the shoes and sell them to the Zedelsky and Syssen families, who would set up shoe shops in Leeds and Manchester respectively. Since they had all been in the shoe business in Lithuania, they knew the requirements of the business. Although not related, they considered themselves as 'family' and were referred to by others as 'the cousins'.

Frank, the eldest Zedelsky brother, had invited Ben to dinner on his arrival in Leeds on Tuesday. He'd insisted Ben stay with them overnight in his family's home in Alwoodly, an affluent district of the city.

'Ben, don't argue. You'll be comfortable, and your dad always stayed with us. It's part of the story! You have now inherited us, and Jane would be most unhappy if you were to break with this tradition.

'Business begins the following morning at eight thirty at head office, where we'll meet with everyone. Come at 6 p.m. – time for a shower and change before dinner.'

That evening, the family table held twelve people. It all seemed very formal to Ben. He had been warned by Frank that Jane liked to see her men in dark suits, white shirts and a not too jazzy a tie. As Ben looked round the table, he saw his three 'uncles' accordingly well dressed, and the wives trim and elegant in their shapely frocks.

He was introduced to Frank's children – his daughter Melissa and her two younger sisters, aged twelve and nine. Melissa was sixteen. Her long dark hair had been carefully and flatteringly brushed and tied at the end with a pretty blue ribbon. She had a warm and smiling face, her lips sculpted into a narrow frame, the nose not too long but nevertheless acceptably prominent. She wore a printed yellow dress which covered her knees. As she helped her mother bring trays of soup to the table and pass them around, Ben noticed that she moved with a certain elan.

Melissa had been given the seat next to him. Ben couldn't fail to notice that they were the subject of interest to the 'aunts' in particular. He intercepted glances between them, and conversation was left quite purposely, he thought, so that Melissa and he could talk more or less privately between them. He was aware, and he had anticipated, that the family would use this evening as an exercise to ensure he and Melissa met in the best of circumstances and would hopefully forge an alliance.

Melissa certainly knew the rules of the game and, without being coquettish, she played her part well.

Ben noticed the deft manner in which she flicked her hair away from her face. He felt the slight touch of her bare arm on his, with apparent innocence as it came into contact with him. Without experience in handling forward-looking girls, he found it difficult to play along with Melissa and was politely quiet and did little to initiate conversation. He allowed her to make all the advances.

'So, Ben, you've taken on a lot of responsibility, I hear! It's great to see you here in Leeds. You should come more often. My father and uncles will give you good reason to come I'm sure, and I will always like to see you,' she said with a warming smile and twinkle of her eyes.

Was Melissa merely playing her expected part with the family? Ben wondered. She wasn't really interested in him, he was sure. She had higher ambitions. He had heard through the family that Melissa was intense in her work, and Ben's mother had never lost an opportunity in telling Ben and his siblings how well Melissa was getting on in school.

'Did you know,' she would say, 'that Melissa has won a scholarship to high school? Her parents won't have to pay any fees, and she's at the best girls' school in Leeds!'

A few weeks later, his mother would remark, 'I hear Melissa's won a scholarship to the Leeds Music College for her abilities on the flute. She really is a remarkably talented girl.'

Melissa had covered herself with academic achievement, getting straight As in her school exams. She was religious in a way Ben clearly was not and had a sharpness of mind and quick wit. Ben knew she did not count him among her thoughts of a long-term partner, and he also knew he was not on the same intellectual wavelength.

She was keen on music; she went to many classic concerts and played flute and viola to a high standard, none of which had interested Ben at any time.

Michael Zedelsky's voice from across the table interrupted Ben's thoughts. 'Tell me, Ben, what's the thinking in London of the possibility of war?'

This was more on Ben's wavelength than the subtleties of Melissa's advances.

'Not good. Nobody cares a damn about the Jews in Germany. Even Kristalnacht last November hardly caused a ripple, although it was well reported in some of the papers – the *Times*, the *Telegraph* and the *Express,* for example. No one wants war, and no one wants to be involved. If it comes, it'll be forced on us. We aren't prepared, and everyone is concerned with another war. If it comes, Uncle, then heaven help us Jews, because no one else will.'

'That's not a good thought,' Michael replied. 'You may well be right, but we ought to be thinking of contingency plans. The army will need boots, more boots and even more boots! Ladies shoes will be curtailed. Leather and ancillary products will be rationed. Everything will be nationalised for the war effort.

'I heard a discussion on this very subject last Tuesday evening on the radio. Some professor of economics, can't recall his name, said this will be one of the first regulations the government will bring in if war is declared.

'We should consider every alternative! We may be too old but you, Ben, will very likely be called up to fight. You must make contingencies with your factory and get your lawyers to protect your interests. We shall all be in a different ball game, and no one will know how it will end.'

'That's a gloomy forecast, Uncle,' Melissa said. 'Surely we can give Ben a little more light in the tunnel?'

'No, Melissa, your uncle is right,' Ben said. 'We have to face what we shall have to face. Recent history is not on our side. The Nazis have taken over the whole of Czechoslovakia. They have taken over Austria. They are threatening Danzig and Poland. We and France are now the protectors of Poland, and if the Nazis attack Poland, there'll be war. If we go to war, we shall be unprepared – as always. Our enemies are armed to the teeth and fully trained and, if the Nazis reach England, then we Jews have no future. I've agonised for months over it. If things get worse, I have it in mind to volunteer for the air force.'

'Surely not, Ben,' Jane said disapprovingly. 'Your duty is to manage the factory. What will happen to your mother and sisters if you're not there?'

'That's for our lawyers to arrange. We have good people in the factory, loyal and knowledgeable. It'll continue to run – if needs be, by making boots as Uncle Mike suggested. I can't avoid my duty if war comes about. Look what they're doing to the Jews in Germany. Do you think those in Austria, Czechoslovakia and now Poland will survive? There are trainloads of children coming in to Liverpool Street Station each week without parents – the trains are known as Kindertransport because most of the children are coming from Germany, Austria and Prague. The children are given homes to go to and they arrive without their parents, whom they may never see again. They do not speak English. They're all Jewish, but many of them have to be placed with non-Jewish families and will now be brought up as Christians. We're in dangerous times and, live or die, I shall fight.'

'Well said!' Melissa applauded. 'But let's hope you'll not be needed.'

ught the conversation to a less serious note by ut the football cup match which Leeds, having wn against Manchester United, was expected to win weekend.

veryone's talking about the match. Most of our staff in eds seem to have obtained tickets. No one talks of anything lse. It's called football fever, and it has attacked Leeds! Jane, I believe Harry Syssen will be visiting for it, a car load of five I believe. They won't be staying. He told me they have to get back for an engagement.'

The evening concluded, fortunately, on this brighter note, and it was well past eleven when the party dispersed to go home to their beds.

'Ben, I suggest seven thirty for a coffee breakfast and we can leave at seven forty-five. I assume you want to be in Manchester by lunchtime?' Frank asked.

Ben nodded and they trooped upstairs, but not before Ben had thanked and kissed Jane on the cheek for the warmth of her hospitality.

'Don't I get one of those?' Melissa asked, raising her voice and eyebrow.

'Of course, cousin!' And shaking off his earlier reserve towards Melissa, Ben planted a strong firm kiss straight on her lips and held her against him for several seconds.

'That's quite enough, young Ben, none of your London romantic cuddles here, please!' said Jane, half reprovingly.

'Ah Mum, you really are a spoilsport. When do I ever get the chance to kiss my cousin?' And with a smirk and a twirl of her skirt, Melissa disappeared upstairs to her room.

***

When Ben returned to the factory, he called Joe Glass to his office. It was plain from the look on Ben's face that all had gone well in Leeds and Manchester.

'Sure,' said Ben in answer to Joe's question. 'We always have a good book in Leeds, and Manchester has taken all the rest we can presently manufacture. They liked our new lines and both approved of the Metropolitan.'

'We need to stack up on our leather skins so we can ensure the manufacturing lines are fully operational,' Joe said.

'Joe, the talk everywhere is of war. In Leeds, my uncles advised we make preparations.'

'What preparations, Bendy?' Joe asked.

'Well, Michael Zedelsky suggested that once war is declared, most businesses like ours are likely to be nationalised, and the government would be interested only in boots, boots and even more boots. He said ladies' designer shoes would be sidelined.

'We must draw up plans so we can change our production and have the most up-to-date and functional boots for the armed forces ready on line. That'll put us in a good position to obtain priority for raw materials. Most of our labour force is too old for active service, and if the factory moves to military requirements, those in administration will rely on us if we can produce the goods to order.'

Ben thought for a moment. 'Also, we should steal a march on our competitors. Let's try to obtain priority from the government for machinery and the raw materials we shall need. Otherwise this factory could dry up if, as I suspect, the items we manufacture now will no longer be needed. Sure, we'll be betting on a coming war, but if anyone really bothers to read Hitler's speeches and follows his actions in Europe, I believe it's inevitable.'

ned to Joe, who had sat silently all through, a ook on his face. 'Joe, keep it close, but you and I pare a contingency plan. I may well be called up, so ing to speak with my lawyers to ensure the factory is and my family are secure. I'm very aware I'm here ause of my father, and he'd have wanted me to look after ny mother and sisters.'

Joe nodded in agreement. 'Good thinking, Bendy. I'll draw up plans for any changes we might need to make. Once we've settled these, why not speak with the war department? Check who's involved in the war production plans and arrange a meeting. They're bound to be impressed if you speak to them before they approach you. At the very least, you'll make the right contacts and, if it were to be settled in an advantageous way for us, we could start the process while keeping our basic production line going.

'I have a feeling you might be first in the field, and it certainly shows patriotism. They'll like that.'

Ben got busy on the phone. He was amazed there seemed to be no particular office or team in charge of any such planning. He was pushed from one department to another and eventually found himself talking to a Mr Hugh Evans, a civil servant in the Home Office, who appeared not only interested in what Ben had to say but positively enthusiastic.

'Mr Bloom, just confirm to me once again. You are proposing to transfer the bulk of your ladies' shoe-manufacturing output to military boot production? You seem to be very clear in your mind that war is imminent. You may, of course, be right. We are making contingency plans, and I would like to discuss your proposal in more detail. Will you call on me on Tuesday next at my offices in Vauxhall? Come at 10 a.m. We're ancillary to the Home

Office in Whitehall, and you'll find us at 202 High Street, Vauxhall. Bring your passport and a sheet of your company's headed notepaper with you. On arrival at reception, ask for me in Room D4. I look forward to meeting you.'

And so it was on 2 May 1939 that Ben found himself on the up escalator at Seven Sisters underground station. He could not fail to notice *her*. She was on the down escalator some twenty feet higher and coming closer by the second. She was slim, with light-coloured hair that ran to the top of her shoulders. On that May morning she was not wearing a coat but a loosely fitting summer dress. She looked happy and carefree, and Ben was immediately attracted to her. She was a little older than him, he thought. Perhaps mid-twenties although, as he held his glance, he thought she looked younger. *She looks a Mary, but she's hopefully a fun-loving Georgina.*

For just a second, before she disappeared from his view, their eyes met almost sublimely, and they exchanged smiles in acknowledgement. Before Ben could look round, though, he had reached the top of the escalator and had to move quickly, being jostled with the crowded early-morning passengers, to his platform. He thought it would be nice to meet her again but considered the chances were less than possible.

And yet the gods play their fateful games.

He found the offices in the High Street without difficulty. He had walked less than five hundred yards from the Vauxhall underground station, having checked the direction with a newspaper vendor at the exit. He saw several imposing red-brick Victorian buildings with large windows on the upper floors – they went up to eight storeys. Ben walked up the stone steps to the dignified entrance of Number 202; the number was built into the headstone at the top of the entrance. He walked across the vast – to his eye – marble-floored hall to the impressive dark teak reception desk which ran the width of the building at the rear. He waited for the elderly white-haired official nearest to him, wearing a dark blue uniform, to attend him.

'I have an appointment with Mr Hugh Evans in Room D4 at ten o'clock. My name is Ben Bloom.'

The official telephoned through to an office. 'Mr Bloom is in reception for Mr Evans,' he announced down the line.

After a few seconds, he replaced the receiver. 'Mr Bloom, will you kindly take a seat over there? A messenger will take you up to Mr Evans when he's ready for you. Have you got your passport?'

Ben produced it, and the official checked that it was indeed his. 'Your passport will be returned to you upstairs,' he said.

It wasn't until after 10.30 a.m. when the messenger in the same dark blue uniform as the receptionist collected Ben – and his passport – and took him up by lift to the fourth floor and along the corridor. Ben saw several people purposefully scurrying to their various offices carrying papers or files.

He was taken into a large office, where the messenger handed the passport to the gentleman behind a huge mahogany desk with green-laid inlay of leather. It stood on an expansive rectangle of a deep red-patterned Turkish rug. The messenger said, very formally, 'Mr Bloom, sir,' and left, closing the door behind him.

The tallish elegant figure, his full head of hair combed with the parting on the 'wrong side'– Hitler-like, thought Ben – rose. He checked the passport, which he then returned to Ben and introduced himself.

'Thank you for coming in to see us, Mr Bloom. I am Hugh Evans and I am deputy director of this department, which carries the responsibility for contingency planning on the home front in the event of war. May I introduce my colleague, Peter Ward?'

Ben hadn't noticed the second man before now. Suddenly very aware of the eloquent and cultured cadences of Hugh Evans' speech, he realised he was speaking with men in authority.

Both men were standing, and Ben shook hands with them. He was ushered to a red-seated chair with gold-coloured wooden back and legs, which stood a metre or so from the front of the desk.

Peter Ward wore black horn-rimmed glasses and had a full head of dark hair, combed back. He was thickset rather than portly and was dressed formally with waistcoat and watch chain across his stomach. He looked to be in his early forties, whereas Hugh Evans seemed to be in his mid-thirties.

Evans paused for a moment, looking at the headed company notepaper which he had taken from inside Ben's passport, where he had carefully folded it that morning.

'So, Mr Bloom, you manufacture ladies' shoes. Our checks indicate you run a successful company and are highly thought of in the shoe business. You are clearly not looking to us to extend your profits, since apparently you have been working for some time at full capacity. You also seem to be very young to have achieved so much. Is your company family owned?'

'Yes, my father set up the company and factory over forty years ago with a person named Tanzer Phillips. Mr Phillips retired before I joined the factory in 1935, but he's still alive. My father died last February.'

Evans nodded. 'So how might you suppose you might be of assistance to us?'

Ben thought he had raised this for the record, since he had already mentioned his suggestion in the phone call.

Evans listened while Ben spoke and then said, 'I have to say, the government has taken no steps so far to organise or co-ordinate mass production of military clothing. Of course, if the fan is to be hit, we shall doubtless move very fast, but it is certainly helpful to have some names on a list and particularly to meet with the director.'

'Well, sir, we all know a war is coming. Sooner rather than later, so everyone believes.'

Evans raised an eyebrow as if to contradict him but remained silent.

'Before that happens, I presume the country will try to prepare and place itself on a war footing. If so, you will require boots – boots for the army and boots for the air force and navy. You won't have enough in stock to give to the millions you will be calling up. So if you want us to change our production line to more of a war footing to meet the demand, we shall need to know in good time.'

Ben received a slight nod from Evans, which he took as an encouraging signal to go on.

'We have to have an agreed style and detail for the boot. We can improve on the 1914–18 model. They have to be comfortable, durable and dry, and we'll have to bring in new equipment and machinery to manufacture them. We'll need priority over leather and raw materials, and we'll need to know sizes, numbers and delivery dates as well as destinations. We'll need to agree on prices. We are not in the market, just in case you were thinking that, to make any profit from this country. The majority of our employees have been with us for years and are experienced. They can change to a new environment quickly without fuss, and most of them are experienced and too old to be called up for active service.

'If this proposal interests your department, then I'll need to know as soon as possible. It takes time to source machinery and the quantity of leather required.'

There was silence.

Finally, Peter Ward spoke for the first time.

'This may well be of interest. It shows commendable initiative, Mr Bloom, on your part to meet with us.'

Evans took up the conversation. 'Mr Bloom, I should like you to prepare a paper outlining the machinery you would require and costings. When we have all this – and if our directorate approves the process – we may be able to set up your factory as a working model. It's still very early days, though. We must see how we go from here.'

'Fine,' said Ben. 'Then at least my journey hasn't been wasted.'

'Certainly not,' Evans reassured him. 'Not at all.' He turned to Ward. 'Peter, may I suggest you arrange a visit to Mr Bloom with Blackett and Dawkins at a convenient time next week?' He turned back to Ben. 'That should give you enough time to set out your proposals and costings in more detail on paper. You can then hand it to Mr Ward and discuss the finer details. I am sure you realise that what has been discussed here this morning must remain confidential, Mr Bloom.'

'Yes, of course, Mr Evans. I expect you realise, though, that my company secretary knows I'm here – and the reasons I came – so I must keep him in the picture.'

Hugh Evans nodded his assent.

Peter Ward took a card out of his wallet and gave it to Ben. 'In case you need to call me. Let's make it 11 a.m. at your factory next Thursday. That'll be May 11th. I shall look forward to meeting you again.'

Both Evans and Ward stood up, bringing the meeting to a formal close, and Ward ushered Ben to the door, shaking his hand most warmly. 'Until May 11th, then,' was the parting comment.

Ben, now unaccompanied, took the lift to the ground floor and, as he left the building, he checked his watch. It was 12.25. He thought he would walk around the Vauxhall area and check out the shoe retailers then have a bite to eat at one of the many cafes in the main street. He'd get back to his factory by about 3 p.m. That would give him time to clear his head, tell Joe what had happened and start drafting the position paper Peter Ward had asked for.

The streets in Vauxhall were busy with women pushing prams or holding children's hands, and other people weaving their way to appointments covered the pavements. Ben didn't think he would win a quiz on the nationalities of the people walking fast past him. The sounds of double-decker buses, vans, lorries and cars added to the busy atmosphere of Vauxhall at lunchtime.

He soon found what he was looking for: several shops selling shoes. He saw Start Right and Charles Wilson & Co and, without going in, he peered at the women's shoes on display set out in the windows. None of them compared favourably with his in terms of quality. His were classier, made better and had sharper lines. Those he was looking at were produced for the cheaper end of the market, but doubtless would sell well in Vauxhall.

He bought a copy of the *Express* and found a seat towards

the back of a cafe. He ordered his usual egg and chips and a mug of tea. 'And please don't forget the ketchup,' he said to the waitress. 'I can't eat chips without ketchup.'

As he browsed through the headlines in the newspaper, he thought about the morning. Was he doing the right thing? He could still pull out. He had great outlets and established retail shops mainly through family. His quality styles had a reputation among the retailers for reliability and saleability. They were always just ahead of the market trend. Should he change a winning team?

But he realised, as he had those few years before at the Battle of Cable Street, that the world was not waiting for him. It was changing – and changing fast. The thought of another European war was abhorrent to everyone. But behind the bland expressions of the people travelling on the underground and buses, Ben sensed a feeling of inevitability. The coming war was against a nation that had invested heavily for the last years in building its army into a disciplined force of millions. Germany had also invested in the most up-to-date armaments.

Ben trusted his instinct. He could not remain inactive. He knew that, come a war, his factory would be taken over by government agencies. It was far better to start proceedings while he had a measure of control. In that sense, the decision had been made for him. He felt an inner confidence that he had been right to contact Hugh Evans.

After lunch, Ben strolled back down the High Street to the underground station and took the Victoria line back to Seven Sisters Road, from where he could walk to the factory.

It was just after 2.30 p.m. when Ben arrived at Seven Sisters station and got onto the down escalator. He was just stepping off the escalator when, to his surprise, he saw the young woman in her summer dress with whom he had exchanged glances that morning. They saw each other and offered hesitant smiles. Ben, never short on initiative, closed towards her and said, 'How remarkable that we meet twice on the same day in the same station! It must be fate.'

The young woman laughed, an easy laugh, warm and friendly.

'My name is Ben. Yours …?' He trailed off.

'I'm Olive.'

'Olive, let me buy you a coffee. That's the least you deserve to celebrate our twice meeting today.'

She laughed again, a sweet laugh free from any embarrassment. 'Why not? I've just finished my stint and have a little time,' she replied.

Ben took Olive gently by the arm and led her out of the station and down the road some fifty yards to a local cafe. It was quiet – just two others sitting at a table by the door.

It was strange, Ben thought. He wouldn't usually have dreamt of inviting a woman he'd just exchanged glances with for a cup of coffee. But it felt so natural to do so.

He leant across the table towards her and looked deep into her lovely eyes. 'Olive, when I saw you this morning, I thought you were the most beautiful girl I had ever seen. You look so fresh and healthy, and so full of life. What do you do that makes you so happy so early in the morning?'

Olive blushed with the compliments. 'Oh, nothing important. I'm working at an insurance firm not far from here – just temporarily. They only require me for six hours a day. It suits me, although I'm looking for a more permanent job.'

Ben thought for a moment. 'If I may ask, what are they paying you?'

'I get four pounds a week, based on six hours a day and a five-day week.'

'Olive, I'm a director of a factory nearby. We manufacture women's shoes. We could do with a full-time administrator or PA in my office. If you can work a full five days, 8 a.m. to 6 p.m. with an hour for lunch, we could offer you nine pounds per week. We don't work Saturdays nor on the Jewish religious days, so there's quite a lot of time off. There's a friendly atmosphere. I think you'd like it.'

Olive looked as surprised as Ben felt. He wouldn't usually be so spontaneous, especially not when the factory was concerned, but something about her felt *right*. He'd known it the minute he'd set eyes on her.

'Sounds good to me,' Olive said. 'When can I come for an interview?'

'This is it, Olive. After coffee, let's walk to the factory. It's about fifteen minutes away. I'll introduce you to Joe – our company secretary – and to others you'll be working with. When could you start?'

'Well, immediately really, as I'm only temporary. I have no contract. They could stop my work at any time and, if I were to call them today, they'll simply obtain another worker, so that's not a problem.'

Just twenty minutes later, Ben introduced his new secretary–administrator to Joe and others in the main office. They fixed up the room adjacent to Ben's, which Olive was to share with the receptionist and telephonist. A sensible-sized desk was brought in together with a Remington typewriter. Joe recorded all Olive's details: home address, telephone number, age and other essentials. She would not, however, give any next of kin, even though Joe had told her it was necessary in case of any injury sustained on the factory premises.

Olive agreed to start work the following morning and used the office telephone to tell the insurance company she would not be returning.

Just after 4 p.m. as Olive was about to leave, Ben explained his business commitment that evening.

'Olive, I'll be working late this evening. We've got an important meeting coming up next week with a government department, and it'll take a lot of preparation. I want to take you out to dinner, but could we make it tomorrow evening? I'll call for you, say, at seven thirty tomorrow. I can get your address from Joe's records.'

'That'll be nice, Ben. I shall look forward to that.'

As Ben bid her farewell, he looked warmly into her eyes, and was met by a mutual response. He could not have felt happier at that moment, he thought, and he could well see that Olive was as happy as he.

'So, until tomorrow then! It has been one of the most interesting and extraordinary days of my life'.

'Mine too,' she replied. With a smile broadening on her face, she turned and left the room.

***

Prompt at 7.30 p.m. on 3 May 1939, Ben rang the bell of 32a Tavistock Avenue, close to Blackhorse Road underground station and just two stops from Seven Sisters. It was a one-bedroom flat with a tiny bathroom, which could just hold a shower cubicle, toilet and basin. There was a kitchenette but no dining area or reception room. He noticed two luggage cases that had carried her worldly goods stacked on top of the lightly constructed wooden wardrobe. The flat was tidy, but Ben noticed how little space there was.

Olive saw him looking around. 'Yes, it's small but it suits my needs. At least it's cheap.'

'So long as you're happy here, that's the main thing,' Ben said.

The flat was less than a quarter of the size of his own, just fifteen minutes away in Beaconsfield Road. Even though his flat also had one bedroom, the rooms were large, the ceilings high and there was a feeling of space. He had a large reception room which doubled as a dining area and a separate kitchen at least twice the size of Olive's. It was clear to Ben that Olive was living in a very tight financial world. But he admired her priorities.

She wore simple clothes which, on her, looked elegant. Her hair had been brushed back into a neat bun. If she released the bun, her long hair would fall to her shoulders. Her skin was fresh, light and as soft as marshmallow. To Ben, she was delightful.

They arrived at Capriccio's, a candlelit Italian restaurant, a little before 8 p.m. Ben had been there a number of times with friends. He had liked the homely atmosphere and the warmth of the service.

The owner and welcoming host, Luigi, was his usual expansive self. Short, distinctly tubby and dressed elegantly in a well-fitting smartly cut suit, he clasped Ben in a warm bearhug. 'Benno, so good to see you!' Releasing him, he looked warmly at Olive. 'And who is this beautiful lady? Your guest this evening?' He gave a rather exaggerated bow while keeping his eyes on her all the time.

Ben introduced Olive and added, 'You see, Olive? You are now marked. You'll not be able to come to Capriccio's without me!'

'That's okay with me, so long as you promise to bring me

here often,' she replied, smiling at Luigi who, in return, clasped her hand on which he planted an expressive, lingering kiss.

'Come, you wonderful people. I have the best table for you,' he said with some éclat.

Olive noticed that most of the tables were for two people.

Having been seated, Ben invited Olive to drink a glass of Sancerre with him and, with her consent, ordered a bottle of Nuit-Saint-Georges for dinner. The lighting was subdued and, notwithstanding the candle on the table, it was not easy to read the menu. They spent time poring over it and exchanged comments before they ordered.

Olive noted that Ben, who was a few years younger than her, was without any sign of the cockiness or arrogance which other men in her life had shown. He was surprisingly easy in his manner, observant to her requirements, polite and really, she admitted to herself, quite charming. She felt comfortable in his company.

The candles flickered, casting a small shadow over their table. Despite the quiet talk from the other tables, Ben and Olive felt alone. As Ben tasted the Sancerre, he relaxed into his chair. 'Olive,' he began hesitantly, 'I want to know all about you. Your childhood, where you grew up, your parents and where they are today.'

'Are you sure, Ben?' she said teasingly. 'You may not like what you hear.'

'Tell me all,' Ben said as he leaned towards her and took her hand across the table. 'I'm a good listener.'

Olive took a deep breath and then began. 'You wouldn't have liked my life. I grew up in a small terraced house in the poorest area in Lime Street. My father worked on building sites, and my mother was a gentle woman. I never understood why they got married, but I guess he had a superficial charm. He was tall and muscular and considered handsome by my mother's friends.'

Olive looked down at her hands and two pink spots appeared on her cheeks. 'He was brutal to my mother and me. He would use his hand – and sometimes his belt – to beat me. I couldn't go out for long periods as I was too embarrassed to let my friends see my cuts and bruises. I left home when I was fifteen. I couldn't stand it any longer. I told my mother I was leaving. She encouraged me, Ben. She told me not to waste my life as she had. "Olive, you go," she said. "Don't let him know where you are. Try to keep in touch with me, quietly, secretly. Don't forget me, Olive."

'I was taken into a convent when I was found on the streets by a passing nun. They were so kind to me. They found me work and taught me religious education, and I was only too pleased to convert to Catholicism. And I remain a strong and loyal believer.'

As Olive set out her life, which got worse as she went on, Ben listened without interruption in rapt attention, soaking up every word she uttered.

'When I was seventeen, I thought I had found real love with a man five years older than me. His name was Arthur Bell and he was also a Catholic, whom I met through the church socials. He was kind at first, but our marriage lasted no longer than eighteen months. I soon found out he was as bad as my father.

'He was hardly at home. He went with other women. If I remonstrated, he would hit me, and then finally he left me for another woman. I have never seen him since, although I occasionally used to see his mother. She was always kind and well knew what I'd had to put up with from her son. I didn't ask where he was and with whom he was living. It was all too painful to me. I moved to this part of London, and here I am, twenty-two years old and still struggling to make ends meet.'

Ben listened thoughtfully and stroked her hand. 'Olive, I know we've just met – we've known each other for less than forty-eight hours. But I must tell you now that I think you are the nicest and loveliest woman I have ever met. However, I do not wish to mislead you. I mustn't become too close to you. I'm Jewish, and it would break my mother's heart – and really upset my family – were I to marry out of the faith.'

Olive smiled and then laughed. 'Ben, no need to worry. I am, as you Jewish people like to say, a chained woman. I am Catholic. My husband is Catholic. He left me, and he doesn't support me. He's living with another woman, and I cannot get a divorce.'

'Why not?'

'The Catholic Church doesn't recognise divorce. I spoke with my priest some months ago, and he told me the only way I could get free to remarry was to obtain a nullity. Strangely, a nullity doesn't rely on wrongful marriage procedures nor on non-consummation of the marriage. It's a legal case which the priest prepares for the bishop, which then goes to the papal nuncio and finishes up in Rome before the curia. It could take many years, and there's certainly no guarantee that it will be granted. My priest even advised against my making any such application.'

Olive smiled sadly. 'So you see, dearest Ben, I am married. I just hope we can remain good friends.'

Ben listened as if in a trance. He had no idea of the Catholic position on divorce and nullity. All he knew was that Olive seemed the very essence of womanhood to him.

He wanted and needed her, and he realised it wasn't only in a carnal way, but also as a warm and close friend. His attraction to Olive had been instant, but he knew his attraction to her could become obsessive. Well, he'd face that problem in due course. At this moment, he was at peace with himself and the world, and this warm, refreshingly beautiful girl was with him.

'Of course we can, Olive. I want to get to know you really well,' he said.

Olive looked into Ben's eyes coyly. 'Ben, I don't believe in love at first sight, but this has been the nearest it's come.'

Ben put his arm around her shoulder as they walked towards his car. As they settled themselves in, Ben leaned over and kissed Olive on the lips, on her face and on her neck. And Olive responded.

5

11 May 1939

Ben had prepared his papers for Thursday's meeting and had spent the morning going over the costings and details of the machinery with Joe. Together, they had decided where the new machinery would be placed and what older machinery they could dispense with. The timings had to be meticulously planned since they could not simply change shoe production completely overnight. There would have to be transitional period where the old production lines could be reduced and the new ones introduced to the labour force. There would have to be a period for change and learning, certainly for industrial safety purposes. But Ben thought the staff capable and experienced enough to be able to adapt quickly to new production lines.

By Wednesday evening, Joe and Ben felt that they'd done all they could. They were ready to submit their proposals to Peter Ward and his team the following morning. *Thank heavens I have Olive*, Ben thought. Her typing at forty words a minute was fast and accurate. She produced several copies of the proposals, all set out expertly and placed in plastic folders for each of the parties who'd be at the meeting.

That evening, Ben had to work late in final preparation for the meeting.

'Olive, I have neglected you. My only excuse is that I have to make careful preparations for our meeting with senior civil servants tomorrow. I really have to get this right. We'll make it up after tomorrow. Can you make Thursday evening?'

'That sounds fine to me. And don't worry, I know this is very important to you.'

Ben nodded. 'It is, but so are you. Thursday evening, then?' He winked. 'Might I suggest you bring an outfit for work on Friday with you?'

Olive flushed and then burst out laughing. 'Is that an invitation to move in with you, Mr Bloom?'

Ben had not thought so far ahead, but it did present the next step in his mind. He was becoming besotted with Olive. Her style, her perfection, her personality, her kindness and her tender love, which he had never before experienced, were having a strong effect on him.

He had noticed that, in the factory, Olive acted totally professionally – no sly smiles; no appreciative comments or touches which could be noticed by members of staff. Ben had had to refrain from touching her as she moved about in his room delivering papers or trays of tea for him and Joe. He had, however, discreetly left a single red rose on her desk most mornings to greet her on her arrival – without a note, but in the sure knowledge she would know who had placed it there.

She had asked about the meeting on Thursday. 'Should I order in sandwiches and cakes, coffee and tea? At what time would you like them served?'

'Yes, that'll be fine, Olive. I'll let you know when to serve them after I've presented the paper. I know three will be coming, but we ought to cater for a fourth in case. Then there'll be Joe and me. I want you in the meeting to take notes, which will have to be typed up afterwards.

'I plan to show the delegates around the factory and introduce them to several of the workforce. Then, back in the office, I'll present my paper and open it up for discussion.

I will want seven chairs around this table with glasses and a jug of water.'

Olive said she would prepare accordingly and draft two of the staff to collect the refreshments. But it would assist if she could know by 11 o'clock latest. He was impressed with her foresight and efficiency and had remarked quietly to Joe that Olive was like gold dust to him as a PA. Ben still felt a little on edge, though. This was *his* policy. He knew, so far as the factory was concerned, it was far-reaching. It would be a major change in production and sales, and he was aware it could go horribly wrong. But he was convinced war was inevitable. He tried to comfort himself with the fact he was probably one of the first in his field to anticipate the problems war would bring to the manufacturing industry.

The meeting went well. Peter Ward introduced Ben and Joe to his two colleagues, Bob Blackett and Jack Dawkins, each dressed in their civil servant suits, crisp white shirts and anonymous ties. Ben guided them around the benches in the factory, introducing them wherever possible to the cutters, stainers and other working staff. He also explained the machinery, and then showed them the dispatch room – the area where the boxes of shoes were prepared for onward delivery. When they returned to Ben's office, the six of them sat around the table and Ben asked whether he could arrange tea and coffee for them. As the discussions on the paper would likely take over an hour, he suggested they could have some sandwiches brought in. This met with approval, and Olive left momentarily to instruct the staff.

Ben guided the delegation through his paper, emphasising a number of bullet points.

'Now I will keep quiet for a few minutes while you digest the detail in the paper,' he said.

The others nodded almost in unison and buried their faces in the documents. It took just a few minutes of civil service speedy reading before Peter Ward started firing off questions. Ben noticed that, apart from Olive, one of the delegates, Jack Dawkins, was also taking notes.

'Once the heads of agreement are exchanged, when can you start? How long will it be until the first delivery of boots can be made?'

Ben gave his answers without hesitation.

'First, we have to purchase the machinery – the details are on page ten of your paper. We can get this into position within three weeks of exchange of agreements. It will take a further two weeks to make all checks and instruct our operatives on their safe working. The design of the boots will have been approved by your department by then and, during the five-week changeover, our operatives will have been trained.

'So, if I say we'll be in full production within six weeks of exchange of agreements, that should be the maximum. Certainly at the beginning, we'll retain a production of twenty per cent output in our ladies' shoes. We can't, as I'm sure you'll understand, simply turn off the tap of supply to our wholesalers and retailers.'

No comment was made by any of the delegation, but Ben was both pleased and relieved to intercept a glance of approval between Peter Ward and his colleagues.

There was further discussion concerning timing. The details for production of the boots were explained – over a period of three months, the factory would be at eighty per cent, retaining a comparatively small shoe production of basic design.

'What will you do if we agree all this and you implement

the plan and then there's no war?' asked Bob Blackett suddenly.

'Then we would all celebrate and, if there were what one might call a permanent peace, we would change back to our peacetime production of making ladies' shoes. It's a judgement which you, gentlemen, will have to make. You'll note on page seven that we have incorporated a clause compensating us in such event. However, I suspect you will need boots for a reserve force even in the event of there being no war. We are not talking of enormous quantities to start with. But the news is so bad now that war seems to be the only outcome.'

'Mr Bloom,' said Peter Ward, 'it may well be that you will be called up. If that happens, who will be in charge of the factory production? May I be frank and ask if the production would work effectively without you?'

'Well, thank you, Mr Ward. That's very flattering. Joe here has been with the company for over thirty years. He knows that I'll be volunteering for the air force if war is declared, and he'll be looking after production. There's nothing he doesn't know about this factory.

'Shlomo, the cutter you met earlier, has been here since 1919, and the majority of our workforce is local and has been with us a number of years. We have here, gentlemen, loyal and hardworking employees. My late father always maintained a family spirit. My absence on air force duty won't compromise quality or quantity of production. This factory works like clockwork and with precision. I only have to conduct the orchestra and, in my absence, Joe here is perfectly capable of taking my place.'

The visitors applauded and laughed.

'Have your lawyers advised you on this paper?' asked Peter Ward.

'Yes, I have seen my lawyers and they have approved it. I've also arranged everything for my probable absence so that I and my family are protected in all events. My mother relies on the income from the shares my late father left to her, as do my three sisters and younger brother, although in their case the shares are few.'

Ben had picked up the vibes. He thought Jack Dawkins and Bob Blackett, who had not been party to the discussions in the ministry and had come new to the situation, were not wholly in agreement with the proposals in the paper. This was probably new to them, and civil servants generally liked to keep to the known and well-used patterns. Change, he realised, was chancy for civil servants. They weren't in the game to take chances. They had their pensions to consider, and their promotions, not forgetting the ladder to national honours and awards. He looked around at their faces to see whether there were signs he could take as approval of the paper. But, at that moment, he could not detect the confirmation he was seeking from the poker-like demeanour of those in front of him.

However, he felt the change in mood when Peter Ward looked around the table at his team and said, 'I believe we have seen what we came for and heard what we had hoped to hear. Mr Bloom, thank you for your time, interest and' – looking at the coffee cups – 'your hospitality. We shall be preparing a report and will discuss this in our department.

'I appreciate you will want to know the answers soon, and we hope to set out our programme to proceed in a few days. Normally, I can assure you,' he said with a smile to his colleagues, 'this operation could take several months. But, as Mr Bloom has so succinctly stated, time is not on our side.

We hope to contact you within a fortnight so please don't join the RAF quite yet!'

They all rose and Ben and Joe shook hands with each person as they left the factory premises.

That evening, at just past 7 p.m., Ben called for Olive at her flat. He had asked her to pack a small case of clothes and toiletries before he took her back to his flat on Beaconsfield Road. No sooner had they entered his flat – they were still in the entrance hall and Olive hadn't even had a chance to put her case down – than he enveloped her in a strong embrace. His hands grazed her neck and unzipped her dress. She responded by gripping his shoulders, and their faces and lips were locked together. It was a manic embrace, which seemed both natural and uncontrollable. Within seconds, Ben had stripped Olive of all her clothes and carried her into the bedroom.

'I didn't know you could be so passionate, Ben!'

'Olive, I've thought of little else today, even during our meeting. When you came in with the refreshments, I thought of this moment, and I have waited patiently ever since.'

Later that evening, after they had showered and Ben had made up a scratch supper in the kitchen of tinned salmon and salad, he put a question to Olive.

'Olive, I know we have only just met but everything is wonderful and I think you feel the same. Why don't you move in with me? There's plenty of room and cupboard space here. We're old enough to arrange our own affairs and it would certainly save you rent and most importantly we would be together. The only problem I can think of is Friday evenings. It's non-negotiable that I am at my mother's house for dinner – it's a Jewish thing. Friday evening has always traditionally been a family evening when my brother Bob and my sisters always come round. It would be impossible to take you.'

'Of course, Ben. I would love to live with you here! Don't worry about Friday evenings. We'll have the other six evenings together. But aren't you worried what people may think? For me, no one knows me or where I come from and I have no problems. But for you, it may be different.'

'Olive, the offer came from me. I'll be more than happy with the situation. Let's agree on this.'

'If it's fine with you, then let's do it. It'll be bliss.'

They held hands, and once again Ben clasped Olive to him in a long lingering embrace.

***

The next few weeks felt like heaven to Ben and Olive. They were careful not to arrive at the factory together, and their conduct during the working week was discreet enough as to avoid any suspicion of their relationship. However, Ben was aware that the truth would seep out somehow. There would be talk, but he and Olive could face that when it happened.

The following Friday evening at his mother's, where Bob and his three elder sisters, Lily, Florrie and Kitty, had also gathered, the weekly greetings were excitedly exchanged. There was always something special about Friday evenings. It was the commencement of the Sabbath. The men always wore their best dark suits, white shirts and smart but not loud ties, and the girls wore pretty dresses, hair well brushed.

'Ben, you look good. Must have been a great week for you,' Florrie said, giving him a hug.

'You're as beautiful as ever,' he replied and quickly added, 'As you both are, Lily and Kitty,' and gave them each a kiss on their foreheads.

'So tell us, what's been so good this week?' asked his mother. She was wearing a traditional Sabbath dark blue dress to the mid-calves of her legs and heavy stockings with smart shoes befitting the widow of a ladies' shoe manufacturer. A string of large off-white cultured pearls hung round her neck, and small diamond earrings completed her Friday evening ensemble.

Ben explained what he was doing with the future of the factory.

'Mum, it's essential for our future that we deal with the Ministry of War production in the Home Office. It's just been set up in the event of war. I was strongly advised by Michael when I was in Leeds to diversify and "get in" with the ministry.

'We'll be manufacturing servicemen's boots. If it all is accepted, we'll have priority for leather. They'll pay for our new machinery, and we'll have a permanent contract with them so long as there'll be war – that's if it comes at all. It won't be as profitable as our present shoe business, but at least we'll be able to keep going and maintain our staff levels. You know how important that was to Dad.'

'Well …' His mother sighed. 'I suppose if *Michael* suggested it, it should be sensible,' she said, leaving little doubt that she would not have accepted Ben's actions if they had not received the seal of approval from the Zedelskys.

They sat round the long dining table in no specific order, except that Ben's mother sat at the top. The rich aroma of roast chicken, potatoes and boiled vegetables reached them from the kitchen. On the table in front of Caroline were two large ornate silver candlesticks, a family heirloom from the mid-eighteenth century in Lithuania. The candles were lit and Ben's mother said the short prayer in Hebrew.

She turned to Ben. 'Ben, you say *Kiddush*.'

Ben picked up the prayer book from the table and, opening it to the relevant page, recited in Hebrew the prayer which had always been the prerogative of his father on Friday evenings; the prayer which brought the Sabbath in to their home.

The Sabbath meal never changed in the family home. Hot chicken soup with *kneidlach*, balls of *matza* meal, chicken fat, chopped eggs and onions with a sprinkling of salt and pepper were all delicious, with which were roast chicken, roast potatoes, swede and parsnips, and concluded with his mother's homemade apple strudel. The traditional Friday evening dinner.

The talk over the table was ill disciplined. It was always the same on Friday evenings, even when Kivi had been there. Everyone, particularly the girls, seemed to speak at the same time. Talking over each other was a customary hallmark of the Bloom family. Kitty, the youngest, was particularly good at this.

'Guess what happened at work this morning –' she began.

But Florrie immediately interrupted her. 'Can't be as good as what I heard went on between the chief accountant and part-time clerk who works half days. They were caught together in the storeroom!'

'Florrie, that's quite enough on a Sabbath evening,' her mother said severely.

It was during this last course that his mother brought up the subject of Ben's joining the RAF.

'Ben, what's all this nonsense I'm hearing about you volunteering to join the air force even before any call-up? I won't have it. Your place is in your father's factory, looking after the family's interests. That's what your father would have done, and that's what he would have expected from you.'

'Mum, you know my feelings towards the fascists. We all know what's going on in Germany. I can't change my feelings.'

'Perhaps not, Ben, but you needn't be the bagel at the top of the bag.'

Ben smiled at the Jewish phrase, despite the topic of conversation.

'Don't volunteer even before a declaration of war. It may never come.'

'Mum, I promise you I'll wait till war comes, as it certainly will, in my opinion. I've seen Solly Teff, who has safeguarded the security of your and the family's interests in the trust he set up for Dad. Solly has always looked after the family. He's a good lawyer and knows what he's doing.'

'I sincerely hope so, Ben. I'll give him a call on Monday. I'll want to know we are all fully protected.'

His mother was agitated at the thought of any possibility of insecurity, and she could not disguise her suspicions. As she spoke, her voice rose in pitch, and her hands and lower arms flew around wildly. Ben did not respond nor react to the implication he might have been pulling the wool over her eyes. He knew it was inherent in his mother's nature to be suspicious of his actions.

The evening ended on a happier note with his sisters competing to take the plates and cutlery to the kitchen, where they washed up and Ben and Bob dried. This was normal practice on Friday evenings. Mother would spend the day preparing, the girls would lay the table and all would clear, wash and dry.

Ben kissed his mother on leaving and gave a hug to each of his sisters.

***

Ben had been growing more anxious by the day. 'Has the post arrived?' he shouted at the receptionist.

'Yes, sir. It went to Joe's office. Nothing addressed to you, sir. You've already told me to hand you any envelope addressed to you personally.'

Ben spoke with Joe, who was calm and seemingly unconcerned with Ben's overwrought attitude.

'Ben, remain calm. They'll tell us soon enough. If it's not on, then we continue and make the best of it. Fretting about it won't help.'

'I know, but I'm anxious about our future. If we stay in shoes, we'll have to reduce our quality styles.'

It was on the following Wednesday morning, three weeks after the meeting, that he received a bulky cream envelope with his printed name followed by his title, director, and the name of the company and address. Marked in big letters across the top were the words 'Private and confidential'. The envelope had been personally delivered to reception, where Olive collected it and signed the receipt for the messenger.

She took it without delay to Ben in his office and did not linger.

Ben paused before opening it. He knew what it contained and from whom it came. He realised that once he opened the envelope staring at him from his hands, he would be opening a new chapter – not only in the life of his father's factory, but also in his own life.

The letter in the envelope was from the Home Office under the signature of Hugh Evans. Ben scanned it quickly and then leafed through the documents that had also been enclosed. They set out the arrangements in contract form, with proposals for immediate advances to purchase the machinery, and also the specifications as required by the ministry. There was also a list of quantities required within four weeks of delivery of the machinery as well as addresses and references for sending the boots onwards. The letter advised Ben to obtain independent legal advice before returning the top set signed. As soon as they were received, an advance cheque would be sent to the company's bank and, from that moment, Ben and his company would be legally responsible for the required deliveries as set out in the agreement.

Ben called in Joe. Strangely, he was not ecstatic as Joe had anticipated. Now the decision had been given, he was strangely calm and very practical. The pair went over the documents line by line. They could see nothing amiss and thought Ben could sign the agreement without amendment. Nevertheless, Ben telephoned Solly Teff and made an appointment for the following morning.

The next day, with Teff's confirmation, the agreement was signed and exchanged.

'Joe, we've actually done it. We're safe! We've protected our workforce, and we've got a march on all our competitors.'

Joe shook Ben's hand many times and clasped him tightly around the shoulders. 'Ben, this is a great achievement. Your father would be so proud if he were here to witness this … You must tell your mother.'

'She knows, Joe, she knows. I'll tell her we've confirmed the agreement. I'll be sure to tell her that Solly Teff gave his approval.'

Ben agreed with Joe that he should now address the work

staff and tell them of the changes in production and the reasons behind the decision. Ben also spoke with his customers, including Michael Zedelsky.

'Michael, I must thank you for your advice regarding a changeover to service boots. I have also taken advice from Solly Teff and have agreed terms with the ministry. We'll be taking on new machinery, and production will start very shortly. This will mean reducing our ladies' shoes, and I'll keep you informed as to production figures.'

Ben's judgement on the question of war proved to be right. During July and August 1939, it became more and more clear that Germany would attack Poland, whose sovereignty had been guaranteed by both France and Britain. The government was making a start in preparing for war. Reserves and territorial forces were called up. Sandbags began to appear in front of government buildings. Air raid shelters were built in public areas, and the home secretary advised the public via the radio to build shelters in their back gardens – specifications were published. These were called Anderson shelters after the home secretary himself. Requirements for the armed forces began taking priority.

Ben felt secure in the knowledge his factory was now in the vanguard and that the agreement he had entered into was being used by the government as a precedent for other companies, which were now being drafted in to a more wartime production.

Olive's move into Ben's flat had worked out well for both of them. They had time together, and there was no longer any formality of having to telephone each other. They were both thrilled to be living together. Ben usually returned to his flat later than Olive, who kept to factory times. They often stayed in during the evenings, listening to their favourite radio programmes. Occasionally, perhaps twice a week and certainly on a Saturday evening, they'd choose to go to a restaurant. Capriccio's remained their favourite.

Ben had spoken to Olive about his intention to volunteer for the air force.

'We must put a stop to the Nazi ideology, and defeating Hitler is the only way. I feel it more as a Jew because I know what's happening in Germany and Austria. It'll be far worse for the Jews in places like Poland should Germany take over. The air force is best for me because I want to fight the Germans, and it's much more direct than being in the army. I'll volunteer for bomber command, so I can see the damage we will inflict.'

Olive was aware she would never win an argument with Ben about joining the RAF. She knew how passionate he was on this subject. It was in his soul and very being. Nothing she could say would change his mind.

'I'll be in training for the first few weeks,' he had continued. 'Then I should be able to come home at weekends or on short leave, and we can be together.'

Olive had no answer to his patriotism and his intentions, which were absolutely clear.

'I promised my mother I would not volunteer until war has been declared. Unfortunately, I believe that will be rather soon. You will, of course, remain with the factory, and I'll have a word with Joe to make sure nothing bad happens to you should they consider changes in staff numbers.

'I'm going to tell him about our relationship. He's got to know, Olive. He's very discreet. He won't gossip. The rent on this flat is paid through my bank, and of course I'll be returning from time to time so you should have no worries on that score.'

'I shall be worried sick when you're on active duty! I just hope I can cope and not let you down.'

Ben gave Olive another hug and said, 'You've nothing to worry about. You know I'm immortal!'

'You shouldn't joke, Ben. You don't need to challenge the gods,' and then Olive added, 'from whatever religion.'

6

Late 1939–early 1940

War was declared on 3 September 1939. On that Sunday morning, Ben and Olive listened to Neville Chamberlain's talk from 10 Downing Street – and his announcement. Ben couldn't help but say, 'Olive, if he had just been stronger with Hitler last year at Munich, this may not have happened. We should have been building up our armaments for years. Churchill was right.'

They gripped each other's hands. 'From this moment our lives will change,' Ben said. 'We'll have to accept it, and much more with the times. Thank God we've got each other.'

'I know, I know. I'm frightened, not for myself but for you, for us, for everyone who will be caught up in this war. I'm frightened for our country.'

'Just continue with your work. It's now war work. We're all in it together now.'

Poland having been savagely attacked and conquered by Germany from the west and by Russia from the east, the war in Eastern Europe seemed to be over by the end of the month. Elements of the British army and air force were moving into northern France, but there was no active fighting. The most the RAF did was drop leaflets on German villages and towns near the frontier.

Ben sought out a recruitment office in Dalston and registered for the RAF. He was told it might take a few weeks before he would be told where to report, and in the meantime he was to go to an office in Wembley for a medical. And then, on 5 January 1940, he received call-up papers to report to RAF Hednesford in Cannock on 20 January for basic training and was given a travel warrant and told what to bring with him.

He and Olive had a last night of tender long embraces and love. She knew Ben would not wish to have a tearful send-off and so she wished him well stoically and gave him a last hug and lingering kiss before he was on his way to the underground station with his case. She knew that, with basic training, he would not be home again for at least six weeks. She had his BFPO address and she promised to write, and he promised to phone her in the evenings when possible.

On arrival at the train station at Cannock, some hundred raw recruits all in civvies and varying modes of dress were met by RAF men with four lorries to take them to the RAF station. They were formally told to line up in three ranks while their cases were thrown into one of the lorries. Ben thought they must all look a curious sight to the public who were present. One old gaffer, who doubtless had fought in an earlier war, said in an audible whisper to his mate, 'Cor, Jack, if we 'ave to rely on these guys for our defence, I think we ought to ask Mr Hitler for peace.'

In reception at the base, their names were checked against the call-up paper they had been ordered to bring with them. They were given a brief medical examination followed by the distribution of uniform, boots (which Ben noticed had not been made by his company), socks, underclothes, tie, shirts, beret, overcoat, raincoat and pyjamas. They then marched, carrying everything, in formation to their billet. Beds were designated and they were told to strip to their underpants and then sent to the showers. Towels had been left for them on their beds, and they put their own clothes in the locker adjacent to the bed.

Corporal Syd Draper was little more than five foot eight, but he nevertheless packed a punch. It wasn't that he was a bully; he just thrived on the power of the two stripes on his arm. The rank of corporal gave him an authority which, in Civvy Street, he would never have enjoyed. His power seemed, to the recruits, to be limitless. He never spoke, he shouted. It was a raucous, unintelligent sound. His vocabulary was limited to a maximum of fifty words, most of which consisted of a repetition of expletives. His larynx seemed not to have been impaired by the continuous noise emanating from his vocal chords. He had the knack, as the recruits were soon to find, of coming within an inch of one's face and shouting at full strength so that his breath and spittle settled on one's nose, in particular, and face in general.

After they had showered, the corporal stripped off a bed.

'Right, you load of shits, I'm going to show how you roll your blankets each morning. I'll only show you once, so you'd better pay attention.'

He moved fast to fold the two sheets and blankets each on top of the other, with the last one binding up the others. It took him less than a minute. It certainly looked a clean and tidy construction.

'Now you there, what's your name?'

'Bobby Sykes, Corporal.'

'No it ain't. You stand to attention when you speak to me. In a loud voice, you state your surname only. This ain't a nursery. We don't go with first names. When you become a corporal, it's just possible that I might be interested to know your first name, but until then – which won't be for some years, and more than likely never in your case, Sykes – you shout your surname immediately. Is that clear?'

Perhaps because he thought everyone had not heard his

loud bark of a voice, he repeated with even greater decibels, 'Is that clear?'

Everyone clamped to attention and shouted, more or less in unison, 'Yes, Corporal!'

'Now, Sykes, since you volunteered, you'll make this bed. You have one minute.'

Poor Sykes, he was all fingers and thumbs. He failed miserably to fold the sheets together in the manner required.

More profanities were screamed at him by the corporal. Then he made everyone strip each of the beds and remake them as he had shown. It took over ten attempts until he began to accept that the finished products were beginning to take shape.

He then warned them they would have to perfect it by the morning if they wanted to taste any breakfast before drill.

'Right, pay attention to what I'm going to say. I won't be repeating myself. Morning reveille is at 0600. We don't waste our time on you lot with a bugle. A bell will ring and you have five minutes to shower, shit and shave. You will then make your beds as I've shown. Inspection at 0620 and you'll be given ten minutes to repair the damage you created. Final inspection at 0630. Breakfast in your working uniforms, polished boots, which you get ready this evening, and on the parade ground at 0650 for inspection. Failure in dress will get you put on fatigue, which will mean extra drill and further inspections.

'If the billet is not in acceptable order, you'll remain until it's approved. This may well mean you'll miss breakfast, as you will be on parade at 0700 for drill. So everything from now on will be at the double, and for the next six weeks. There'll be no sauntering, no slackness. I want enthusiasm at all times and, if I don't get it, you'll find I'll be right behind you.

'If, at the end of this six-week course, you've been approved by the sergeant and officers, you'll get a forty-eight-hour leave pass with warrants and then have to report to your next base for more specific trade training. It'll be during this course that your first selection will take place for your onward trades, whether it be flying operations, engineering, maintenance or whatever.'

The corporal looked around with a menacing stare.

Most of the recruits were in shock. Ben had been expecting the loud-mouthed vapourings from the corporal, but neither he nor his mates expected the constant stream of invective directed at them. No one would dare to comment or challenge. They accepted their present plight and simply looked down at their boots. They didn't move their feet; they kept still and silent.

'If you think I might be tough,' the corporal continued, 'then you haven't heard Sergeant Makins. He'll inspect the billet tomorrow morning, and I'm telling you it had better be in real shipshape order or you'll never know what hit you. If you think this is tough, then you'd better understand that, across the water, the young Jerries are going through the same sort of training but probably harder. You'll be competing with them when you're fully trained, so you lot better get your bloody skates on.

'Those who fail will be placed in a more disciplined squad for retraining. It'll be another forty-two days without leave. I'll tell you this: you won't want to be in retraining.'

Ben had thought he had known what to expect and accepted that he would endure whatever was placed before him. He had volunteered, which was rare among those he was with, and so was more prepared for the shouting, profane language and physical tests.

In the preliminary interviews with a flying officer, he was asked what trade he wished to apply for. His CV, which everyone had had to complete in detail, was in front of the officer. Ben said he wanted to volunteer for bomber command and thought he would be best suited as a wireless operator, but he would accept being a gunner if necessary. All this was noted but nothing was said to suggest his request would be accepted.

The days were taken up with drills, more drills, cross-country runs, circuit training and parades with uniform inspections in which everything had to be shining and clean. Boots had to be polished mirror-like, belts and webbing had to be blancoed to perfection with shining brassware attached and trousers pressed so the creases were stiff. Ben – and the others – soon learned that candle wax heated and ironed into the creases of the trousers gave them a sharp appearance, which helped to impress the inspecting sergeant.

They missed a number of breakfasts, or were so late that they only managed to get a cup of tea down before appearing on the parade ground. Shouting was endemic. No NCO spoke to you; they shouted inches away from your face or ear. But no one cracked up under the intense strain, and everyone knew that military discipline had to be drummed into them so their actions became second nature to the commands given to them.

Within six weeks, the platoon was working as a disciplined unit. All were now working together and helping each other. There was no competition between them. Friendships between the recruits strengthened, notwithstanding the fact that few had much in common. Nicknames were conjured up from nowhere, and Ben became known as Bendy.

Towards the end of this initiation course, Ben felt he had never been so fit. He felt light on his feet and moved with an athletic feeling of physical power and alertness.

'Christ, this bloody food is so boring,' moaned Hooky Clapper, formerly a first-year clerk with an insurance firm in Heaton in Yorkshire. He spoke with a broad Yorkshire accent. Known as Hooky for most of his life due to the prominence of his nose, he was chirpy and talkative. He was popular because he could never stop making funny asides and kept himself just onside with the NCOs. 'Bloody chips all the time, and the peas are so hard they could be fired from Spitfires and do real damage to Messerschmitts.'

'What do you expect, silver service at The Savoy? This suits me. I like chips with everything,' Will Evans answered.

'Well, everything will be better than from where you come,' Hooky fired back, knowing Will came from Criccieth, deep in Wales.

General laughter and agreement completed the badinage, and conversation moved on to more serious stuff about when they might be allowed to team up with some girls. Not being allowed off camp, there had been no feminine company to be seen.

'I can keep with the order, discipline and being continually shouted at, but I can't do without a chick on my arm. I miss the girls,' Hooky said with a sigh. 'If I have to do a re-course for another six weeks, I'll go absolutely mad. I'll even go AWOL if I have to, but I can't do with only male company for another session.'

During this time, telephone calls had not been permitted. There were no public telephones in the camp and the recruits were never allowed in any office where telephones were, as they were used exclusively for operational purposes. Nor had there been any post delivered, so Ben had not heard from Olive and could not contact her. He wondered often how she was coping but knew in his mind that she would be fine. No news was good news to her, she had told him. So his mind was at rest.

He had been spurred on by the friendship and comradeship created by the common ground in which all of the recruits found themselves. There was a spirit of teamwork where everyone would help each other if there was a problem. There was no individual competitive spirit, but the drilling and the billet-cleaning in particular required total mutual support, which was deliberately fostered by the NCOs and the system in place. People Ben would never have known otherwise and who were not part of his social group became close friends and, by the end of the six weeks, he felt he would be only too pleased to meet with them in Civvy Street when the war was over.

'Bendy, what makes you want to be in bomber command? Dangerous living, you know,' said Alf Wotton, an apprentice plasterer from Wigan.

'Simple, Alf – I volunteered to join before call-up. I just want to get at the Huns. It's the best way for me to be in the fighting.'

'Well, you won't find *me* volunteering for anything except demob. I'm hoping to be alive at the end of this caper. If I can find a cushy number, that'll be fine with me. I'll do my work, but I'm not one for the front line, if I can help it!'

'Each to his own. Let's have a beer-up when all this is over. It could take a year or two, though!'

'And the rest, Bendy. God knows when this will be over. I tell you what. Let's make a promise to meet up at the Flask at Highgate a week after demob or the date the war ends.

We'll exchange addresses before we leave this dump. I'll drop you a line. The Flask in Highgate is my cousin's favourite pub. I occasionally stay with him. I can really recommend it.'

'That's fine with me. I don't know the Flask, but if you remind me when you get in touch, I'll find it. That's a promise, and it's something to look forward to. Get some of the other lads to join us, particularly Fred Green and Curly Davies. God, I'm already drinking the pints in anticipation,' Ben said, licking his lips.

7

5 April 1940

There were three unfortunate recruits who failed the course and were retained for a repeat. But Alf and Ben were not among them, nor were Hooky or Will Evans. At last, Ben was able to telephone Olive to tell her that he had one week's leave and would be at the flat by 7 p.m. He had to travel in uniform and take all the clothes he had brought with him in a large shoulder bag.

He had been interviewed just prior to the passing out parade by the squadron leader, who was in command of the sections; he was the highest ranking officer Ben had seen in the whole time he had been at RAF Hednesford. He'd been told that he was to report to RAF Compton Bassett on 16 April and had been given a warrant and an order paper which he would have to present when he arrived. There, he had been told, he would undergo a six-week course on electrics, receivers, transmitters and aerials; in fact, it included everything required for passing out as a qualified wireless operator, which was exactly what he had wanted.

Ben arrived at his flat, just as he had planned, a little after 7 p.m. on Friday, 5 April. At the small florist shop close to Seven Sisters underground station, he had bought as large a bouquet of flowers as he could carry. He opened the front door and, before he could carry in his heavy shoulder bag and the flowers, he was embraced by an excited Olive, who threw her arms around him. She guided him into the bedroom while stumbling over his baggage.

'Olive, let me get in! Let me get rid of all this clobber and then I can hug and kiss you as hard as you like.'

Olive was so delighted to see him. The six weeks of absence had strengthened the bonds between them. Ben had greatly missed her – her humour, her kindliness, her affection towards him, her hair, the delicacy of her skin. Now she was here, in front of him, looking as beautiful as he had remembered, and as he had dreamt every night. The genuine warmth of her welcome all but overpowered him. It was clear to Ben that Olive felt the same towards him. They could hardly wait to clear his baggage and, together, take off his uniform. They fell on to the bed and wound themselves around each other.

'It seems I've been waiting for you for so long, Ben! You look so handsome. You've lost weight and you look so fit. You're *my* man. There never could be anyone else.'

'Olive, I feel the same with you,' Ben murmured, gently kissing her nipple. 'This, Olive, is what I call a homecoming.'

And they lapsed into a more quiet passion, clinging strongly to each other.

Monday, 8 April 1940

Joe had readily agreed Olive could take a week's leave to be with Ben. No one else in the factory had an inkling as to her relationship with Ben. He arrived at the factory in his uniform at 9.30 a.m., giving time to everyone to have settled into the work mode. As he walked down the lines of the work benches, he was met with cheers, greetings and good wishes for a safe RAF career. He talked with groups of employees, accepting the proffered hands, returning smiles and countering the warm words of support given to him. He clasped Shlomo to him warmly.

'Ben, I'm so proud of you in your uniform. You make sure you'll kill the Jerries and you make sure they don't kill you. You're worth more than any of 'em.'

'Thanks, Shlomo. I've always tried to do what you advised me to.'

They gave each other another hug before Ben settled down with Joe in the office.

'It's like clockwork, just as we had planned,' Joe said. 'The ministry has kept to everything they agreed. The new machinery has all arrived. Payments were made in time to cover all the costs. It didn't take too long for our people to start using the new machines safely and effectively. The boots coming off line are good quality, and the ministry seems to be very pleased with us. Deliveries are weekly and there's now an accepted pattern.'

Ben nodded and indicated Joe should continue.

'We haven't lost all our retailers for our women's shoes, but it's now down to thirty per cent production and will settle at fifteen per cent by June. Our customers in Leeds and Manchester have diversified and have changed their specifications to more popular and modest lines in view of the war. So far, we've had few difficulties. Sure, we've had the occasional teething problems. One of the new machines didn't work and we had to call in the manufacturers. They found our operatives had failed to clear the roughage which collects from the cutting and it had blocked the outflow channel. A bit embarrassing, but we can get over such blips.

'We get phone calls from some retailers begging us to let them have deliveries and we have to fend them off by allowing them a few boxes here and now. We don't want to cut off our retailers if we can avoid it. Keep as good relations as we can – that's our present motto.'

Ben listened closely and then clapped his hands together. 'This is good news! You've done well. You've seen the factory through some demanding changes in challenging times and have kept a happy workforce. I expect profits will be down, but that'll be the result of greater austerity from the government and a reduction in sales of our high-quality shoes.'

Ben was fully aware the ministry would only agree to a price lower than the private sector. However, while there was a war, they needed to keep the business alive, keep their employment up and assist the war production.

Ben returned to the flat just after midday. Olive had prepared a packed lunch to take with them on a picnic she had mentioned earlier in the morning.

'Change into casuals and you need a sweater,' she said. 'It's none too warm. I thought we could go to the countryside in the car. Perhaps in the Epping area. There are good walks around with a pub or two as well.'

'Great! Is there petrol in the car?'

She laughed. 'Ben, I don't drive! The car hasn't been used for the last six weeks. But the petrol stations are still open. They haven't brought in rationing yet, but they're talking of creating coupons.'

'I don't think I really need a car. I won't get too many leave passes, and I certainly won't be able to have time to use the car where I'm going. It'll simply rot away here. I might as well sell it. But today, we drive!' he said emphatically.

Olive was right. It wasn't warm but there was sun and a blue sky. They found a quiet layby in a country lane to park in.

As they lay on rugs, having an early lunch, Ben was struck by the fact Olive had not forgotten to bring a bottle opener for the beers. She was perfect in every way, he thought. He leaned over as she was depositing salad on plates and gave her a kiss on the nape of her neck. She turned quickly and returned the compliment on his lips. As the lunch plates, full with salad and fishcakes, waited, they fell into a closeted embrace.

During their walk, Ben told Olive he thought they should move out of London.

'Now that Hitler has disposed of the Poles, the talk is he will attack in the west. If he does, like in Poland, he'll send his Luftwaffe over to bomb us. If it's anything like what happened in Poland, and Warsaw in particular, London will be under continuous air attack. I want you safe. I don't want to come back to a ruined house and find you in hospital. Or worse.

'I've checked a few things out and think we can find a single-bedroom flat similar to the one we have at present but in the countryside. Somewhere like this near the Forest of Epping. It should be safe here. No industry and no air stations to be bombed. You'll have to find a job there, but with your capabilities that shouldn't be difficult in wartime with so many people away in the forces.'

'If that's what you want, Ben, I won't object. Have you anywhere in particular in mind?'

'Well, Epping seems a good place, not far from London. It might make it more difficult to visit my mother, but I'll have to work on that. We can easily pick up a flat through the agents there. I heard there are many vacant properties at the moment and the rent won't be high. Let me deal with it tomorrow and we can give notice on our flat at the same time.'

Later in the early evening, Ben telephoned his mother and found she was well but, as ever, moody.

‘So Ben, you couldn’t have spoken to me earlier? You’ve been home two days and I’ve had to wait to hear from you.’

She hadn’t asked how he was or how he had got on in the RAF. He was aware, though, that his mother would never think of asking him about his life or work. He had never mentioned Olive to her.

‘So when will you come and see me?’ she enquired, her tone suggesting Ben hadn’t considered her at all.

‘Well, Mum, if the family are coming on Friday evening, perhaps that would be best so I can see everyone at the same time.’

‘Oh I see, you’re here for a week but you can only see me for one evening?’

‘I was in the factory this morning and I have to see a number of people. Best time for both of us is Friday evening. I’m back on duty early on Monday. Will that be okay? If it’s not convenient, I can make it another time.’

‘Thanks for fitting me in with your engagements, Ben,’ she said sourly. ‘Yes, I suppose so, Friday at 7 p.m. as usual. They’ll all be here, wanting to see you. Don’t come in uniform. It’ll upset me. You should never have volunteered. Don’t know what you were thinking of when your father’s factory needed you.’

‘Okay, Mum. See you Friday. Must go.’ And Ben put the phone down.

Olive knew he would have to be with his family on Friday evening, and she also knew that Ben could not take her with him.

***

Friday evening was not the disaster Ben thought it might be. His sisters and Bob were all agog at his news of the recruit training he had undergone. He made the point, mainly for his mother, that, had he not volunteered, he would have been waiting in suspense for his call-up papers, not knowing when it might happen. As it was, he had had time to organise his departure from the factory.

His sisters all had good jobs which kept them busy and financially independent, and Bob, making his way in insurance, was expecting *his* call-up papers at any time.

'I'll almost certainly be in the army,' he said. 'They'll place me without giving me any option. I don't think I have any special skills, except perhaps admin. The one thing I don't want is the navy. I can't swim, and I'll be continuously seasick.'

'Well, Nelson was always seasick when he went aboard his ship and he didn't do too badly,' Florrie said.

'Florrie, don't be perverse! Bob isn't Nelson. I hope he'll be a pen-pusher in the home army. Best we can hope for. I don't need the worry that Ben is giving me! Just keep out of trouble and don't volunteer like your brother,' said his mother, turning towards Bob.

Conversation petered out at this moment, but Florrie was quick to intervene.

'Right, Ben, you clear the table with Bob. Kitty and I'll do the washing up. You men can help with the drying.'

There was suddenly a great deal of activity, with Ben and Bob coming and going laden with the used crockery, cutlery and wine glasses. The table was cleared and the cloth taken off and, as it was spattered with drops of wine and stained with gravy, it was placed in the washing tub for the following day's wash. Chairs were replaced around the table and the total disorder at the end of a Friday evening dinner made way for a fresh-looking room.

Kitty had swept the carpet and, by the time the drying

up and the putting away of the crockery had been completed, the room looked ready to be laid again.

The clearing up had been the pattern for many years since they had been young children. Mother had cooked the dinner and then it had been up to the children to lay and clear up.

The sisters surrounded Ben as he was leaving. 'Ben, you look after yourself, No heroics. We want you alive at the end of this war,' Florrie ordered as she gave him a peck on the cheek.

'So I will, and so do I,' Ben replied playfully to all, but looking at Florrie.

As he stood on the doorstep, Ben shouted back to his mother, 'Thanks once again for another great dinner. I'll keep in touch when I can. Love you,' and he was away.

On his way back to his flat, Ben reflected on the evening's dinner. He had always known his mother was not an easy woman to relate to. He had never resented her closeness to his sisters rather than to him and Bob. But he was finding her regular barbs and criticisms of him a growing irritation, and he was finding it more difficult to restrain himself from giving a sharp response. But he knew he could never win a verbal battle with her. She was his mother. He owed respect to her, particularly now his father was no longer around.

He hadn't mentioned his proposed change of address – which he had arranged a few days earlier – to his family. He knew he wouldn't have been able to control the conversation, and there would be many questions as to why and as to the location. He hadn't wanted to dig a hole for himself or not sound genuine. Better, he thought, not to say anything at this moment and let matters fall into place later.

He and Olive had visited Epping on the bus and had seen

some flats. They had chosen one near to the Forest in Chingford Mount. It had a beautiful outlook and was in a quiet and peaceful area. Olive would have to give Joe a week's notice, but she had also obtained information from the helpful letting agent and had heard that a local firm of solicitors were looking out for a receptionist and general administrator. That was exactly what Olive was hoping for. The pay was less than she was earning in the factory, but Ben agreed she could not expect the same wage as in London and, after all, it was cheaper living in the countryside.

Accompanied by Ben, she had applied there and then and, without too much delay in the interview, she was given the post to start in two weeks' time.

It was close to midnight when Ben returned to the flat, relieved and delighted to find Olive awake and reading in bed waiting for his return.

8

18 April 1940

Along with some twenty others, Ben arrived at RAF Compton Bassett for his wireless operators' course. He knew that this was an intensive course over four weeks learning how to use the R1155 receiver, the T1154 transmitter, the A1134 crew intercommunication amplifier, the aerial switch type J, proficiency in Morse code and the Morse key type F, the aerial ammeter, the aerial capacitor, the Fishpond indicator unit type 182A and the calibrator crystal monitor. There were regular tests, and those who didn't pass had to retake them within forty-eight hours, so a lot of midnight sweat went on. If an airman could not pass the course, he was weeded out and reposted.

Ben found the course fascinating. He lived and breathed every moment of it. It was exactly as he had hoped. He had had no wish to be a tail gunner nor a bomb aimer, although he would have accepted that if he had not been able to pass the wireless operators' course. On the dot at 0800 hours, everyone would crowd into Hut C for the first of many daily lectures. Armed with his manual, Ben eagerly wrote his notes and listened attentively to the instructors. He excelled at his work and took to Morse code as if he were an excited schoolboy learning in the Scouts – of which he'd never been a member.

Due to his ability to speak Yiddish – he'd picked it up from his parents and their friends when he was first learning to speak – the officers considered he had sufficient knowledge of German to be able to operate the ABC equipment. This stood for Airborne Cigar, which was a radio countermeasure. Ben was trained to scan for German night-fighter radio frequencies. Once he'd located the frequency, he had to tune in one of his several jamming transmitters on board the aircraft to that frequency and thus prevent further information being transmitted to the night-fighter pilots by German ground transmitters.

As a contrast to the atmosphere on his basic training course, the radio in the canteen was always on, blaring out music. They all went with the songs of the day and the great favourite, who received a cheer whenever she was played, was Vera Lynn, who was introduced by the presenter as 'the Forces' Sweetheart'. Her signature tune was 'The White Cliffs of Dover' and when she sang it everyone would join in. The mood from the serious life of learning was considerably lightened.

Ben enjoyed the fellowship of his new friends. He thought they were generally a more intelligent group than those on basic training. But because of the intensity and technicalities of the course, there was little time for the chat and badinage that Ben had experienced at RAF Hednesford. They all had to pass this course, and there was much swotting in the evenings in preparation for the next test. Most smoked while they read, and there was little time to make lasting friendships.

Ben passed the course with flying colours and was congratulated by the commanding officer, Squadron Leader Emery. He was given a forty-eight hour pass and told Olive he would be coming home. He also telephoned his mother to tell her he had passed his course successfully. He told her that he didn't have time to visit but was pleased to hear that all was well and that his sisters still visited on Friday evenings. Bob had been called up and was doing his basic training in

Portsmouth in the navy. *Well*, thought Ben, *that just shows Bob's preferences stood no chance during wartime!*

His mother asked him to visit her when he could but, for once, she seemed to realise his duties did not make this easy.

Early in June 1940, Ben was posted to Conversion Course Number 1664 at Doncaster to fly Halifax Bombers. When he arrived, he soon heard from the buzz in the mess that the Halifax was not a safe aircraft to fly. There had been a number of recent crashes resulting in several deaths due, it had been said, to mechanical problems. The Halifax was referred to as 'the coffin-maker' in the mess.

The airfield was huge to Ben's eye. This was not an operational station. Ben could see ten Halifaxes standing on the field some hundred yards from the hanger buildings. Four other smaller planes, which Ben could not identify, stood nearby. There were maintenance men busying themselves around three of the planes and crossing to and fro from the hangars. They were under the supervision of a sergeant and one officer.

For the first time, Ben saw the WAAFs in their uniforms under the guidance of WAAF NCOs and an officer. He also noticed the informality in uniform dress and a casualness among the maintenance men. Here, there was no spit and polish. They were workers doing their job. No shouting of orders like in the army or navy. Here was the junior service at work, no continuous saluting or stamping of boots on the tarmac. Ben realised the RAF was more democratic, and not steeped in the tradition of rank.

He was soon back to reality after his moment of daydreaming. The teams had already been selected, with Pilot Officer George Makins, Sergeant Nick Mosby, the navigator, Mick Giffin, the flight engineer, and three others – and Ben as the wireless operator. Their first training flight was with Flying Officer Jock Wood.

It wasn't helpful for morale when he said, after Ben and the rest had climbed into the plane, 'I'm going to show you that the Halifax is quite safe despite all the crashes this week. There have been five crashes. They've all been due to pilot error.'

With the background of the tainted reputation of the Halifax Bomber ringing in his ears, Ben was not alone in feeling queasy when finding his seat on this first flight. Like the others, he had to crouch down as he moved slowly along the fuselage to his seat with all the radio equipment immediately behind the navigator.

God, if I feel like this on the so-called 'dummy run' how will I cope on active service? he thought.

'Get a grip, Ben,' he said quietly to himself. But it took some twenty minutes for him to be able to relax and concentrate on his wireless.

Jock revved up the engines. The noise was horrific. Ben tightened his hands on the radio desk in front of him. He checked his harness straps, which confirmed he was securely strapped in. The Halifax rolled on to the tarmac and then, with a burst of high-pitch volume from the screaming engines, moved with increasing speed down the runway.

Jock took the plane up to ten thousand feet. With the Halifax flying above the clouds, Ben was amazed to see the white puffs and larger balloons of cloud passing under him. If it weren't for the adrenalin pumping into him with his concern over the reliability of the aircraft, he might have enjoyed the experience more. He reflected that, if Jock was relaxed, *he* should be too. But he knew he wasn't. This was his first ever flight on an aircraft and he was ashamed he felt as if he was going to be sick. He kept his mind on the radio frequencies and practiced what he had learned at Compton Bassett – anything to prevent him from being sick. He knew that would be the ultimate humiliation, and he would be the butt of jokes for the rest of the course. Fortunately, he was able to stave off the queasiness.

Jock turned to Mick Giffin, the flight engineer, and said, 'When I say do it, do it straight away'.

Mick nodded. Within thirty seconds, Jock shouted above the roar of the engines, 'Cut the starboard outer engine.' Mick did so. Less than a minute later, the order came. 'Cut the port outer,' which Mick, again, did straight away. All the time he was piloting, Jock was talking to the crew. Next, he ordered, 'Cut starboard inner.'

Ben and the crew said nothing, but the plane was flying erratically because they were flying on only one engine.

Jock shouted above the noise of the engine, 'See, this Halifax is quite safe. It'll fly on one engine!'

Ben prayed Jock would not try to prove this, but Jock turned back to the flight engineer. 'Now be quick when I tell you to start the engines up. And cut the port engine. You see, guys, we are still flying. We are losing height, but we are gliding.'

A few seconds later, Ben was relieved to hear the order, 'Right, start the port inner and start the starboard outer,' and within seconds all four of the plane's engines roared.

Jock shouted above the noise, not without a certain triumph in his voice, 'You see, boys? The Halifax is quite safe.'

They came in to land and, having done so, Jock turned to George, the pilot on their course, and said, 'Right, George, now it's your turn.' They swapped seats and had a bit of a discussion before George took off.

Jock turned to Mick Giffin. 'You did one thing wrong when we were doing all these actions.'

'What was that, sir?'

'When I got down to one engine, I put some boost on. You should have stopped me. You should have tapped my hand and knocked my knuckles and brought down the lever to take the boost off.'

'Oh, right, sir,' said Mick, obviously knowing full well he would not have dared to do any such action to his superior officer, who at that time was flying the plane. But he had learned an important lesson from this advice.

George took them around the circuit, landed and took off again. Each time he landed, he bounced a few times.

'Don't worry about these bumps on landing,' Jock said. 'This guy can certainly fly! He's done everything I've asked of him.'

He turned to George. 'I'll fly with you once more on a cross-country trip then you'll be able to fly on your own.'

During this further flight with Jock sitting next to the pilot, Dick Sheppard, the bomb aimer, opened and closed the bomb doors, and the gunners fired off a number of rounds from the new type of gun turrets – there were two on a Halifax. They also had electric sights, which took a bit of getting used to. Ben worked his wireless to get fixes; Nick, the navigator, was sitting next to Ben and asked him to get a fix on RAF Aldergrove for him, which Ben did. A number of other fixes were obtained, and Nick showed Ben his map and said, 'That's where I planned the route and we're bang on course.'

***

Fourteen days later, having completed the course, Ben and the others were given seven days' leave before they were posted to an operational Halifax squadron. He telephoned Olive to tell her he was coming home. 'That's wonderful, Ben! I'll prepare a homecoming for you immediately. I'll try to get some time off, but I haven't been at this job long so it might not be possible.'

'Don't worry, darling. I'll have to visit my mother and also see Joe in the factory. We'll just make up for it in the evenings. See you soon. Love you.'

Ben arrived home at midday on Saturday. Olive had prepared a large summer salad followed by a selection of fresh fruit for his homecoming. The lunch was complemented with a bottle of cool Sancerre to recall their first dinner at Capriccio's. They celebrated their reunion by listening and dancing to their favourite tunes on the HMV record phonograph before Olive led Ben into the bedroom.

They left the house at just a little after 7 p.m. and headed to a cosy restaurant in the town.

'I miss you, Ben,' Olive said over dinner. 'I think about what you're doing all the time.'

'That's not good. Your boss expects you to concentrate on your work, and that's more important. I'm all right. So long as I've got you, nothing can happen to me.'

'Don't say that! I'm superstitious. Don't challenge the gods …'

During the week, Ben visited his mother – but not in uniform.

'I'm glad to see you,' she said. 'You look fit and well. They must be feeding you well. I worry about you,' she added, as if to excuse herself from saying he was being looked after. 'Mind you, we're more in the war in London than you are! Bombing every night – I have to go to our shelter in the back garden. It's all very worrying. No one knows how all this is going to end.'

'I know, Mum. Why don't you move in to the countryside? You'll be so much safer. You've no need to live here in danger.'

'I'm not going to move, Ben! Let that dreadful Hitler make me move from our family home? Certainly not. The girls have been called up too. Lily is in the Wrens and hopes to be sent to Portsmouth where she can see Bob. Florrie and Kitty are in the army. The ATS, I believe it's called. They're on basic training now. They won't be on the front line and will be secretaries or something, so I'm not going to worry too much about them.'

Ben's visit to the factory was a good deal warmer. He did not go in uniform this time, but he was able to talk to all the workforce as he made his rounds and ask them how they were managing the bombing at nights. They were all cheery and so pleased to see him.

'Give 'em hell, Mr Bloom! Better than they're giving us. Don't spare the bastards. Drop as many bombs on them as you can,' was the general refrain. He countered their good wishes with his own good wishes for their safety and for their families.

Joe had good news for him. 'We remain on course,' he said. 'The inspector gives us high marks, and we are getting what we need in leather.'

***

When Ben arrived at his new Halifax squadron, he found himself with the same crew. It was usual for the pilot to choose his crew, and George had wanted the same guys as on the course to be with him. Ben was very happy about this, as they had forged themselves into a good team on the Halifax course.

During the next two and a bit years, between late 1940 and early 1943, Ben completed his tour of thirty operational sorties. Many of these had been over Germany but, in the early period, they had been over the channel ports in France, bombing the build-up of German naval troop carriers for the threatened invasion of Britain. Their plane had to be repaired from time to time due to the flak which had torn into it. But they had been fortunate and, although there had been comparatively minor injuries sustained from fragments of incoming shells, no one had been seriously wounded.

On completion of the tour, the crew was broken up and assigned to non-operational units as instructors to give them a rest. It was not however, uncommon for a rested crew member to volunteer for a second bomber tour. And that is exactly what Ben did.

He had made it clear to his commanding officer that he had no wish to become an instructor. He had come to fight the battle, and he wanted to continue. His decision was accepted and he received a promotion to sergeant, which meant not only higher pay membership of the sergeants' mess with better food but also, without being too snobbish, better and more intelligent company. He was given a twenty-one day leave pass to celebrate.

9

February 1943

At last, Ben could spend some quality time with Olive. He'd only seen her fleetingly when he could talk himself into a forty-eight-hour pass or even just a thirty-six-hour one. He had been able to get leave for five days over Christmas in 1942, when he and Olive had snuggled up together for most of the time in bed; it was the warmest place to be in an otherwise freezing winter. He had badly needed the rest then. He hadn't realised that the pressures of night-flying over enemy territory had the effect of creating a mental tiredness which he seemed unable to overcome. Now he had a twenty one day leave and had arrived at their house in Chingford Mount late afternoon on the Friday. Olive was still at work.

He was exhausted. At the operational station, they'd kept going on a combination of adrenalin and cigarettes. They couldn't afford to relax for a minute on operations. Now back at home, it was as though his body was trying to catch up.

'Olive,' he said down the telephone, 'I'll have to see my mother, and it's best if I do so on Sunday over lunch. Friday evenings are out because it's impossible to get back late at night to Chingford Mount.'

'Fine, Ben. That's probably best. I'm so looking forward to seeing you. I'll be home a little after six.'

He rang his mother. 'Mum, can I see you over Sunday lunch? It'll be too late to come over tonight, and I've given you no notice.'

'I can't see why not. I'm having your sisters over then, and they've asked me if they can bring their boyfriends. I'd like you meet them. They seem very nice to me, but I'd like your opinion, Ben.'

'Sure. It'll be good to see everyone. I take it Bob won't make it then?'

'No, he's on a destroyer. Don't know where, of course. Don't suppose he does either. It seems both my sons are in danger. See you Sunday, then. Come at twelve thirty.'

'Okay, I'll try to be on time.'

When Olive arrived home at just after quarter past six, Ben saw she looked so wonderfully bright and full of health.

She seemed to have put on a little weight. Her face was a tad fuller and her smile, so engaging to Ben, seemed larger than he recalled.

'Ben, it's just so wonderful to have you home! My boss agreed to give me two weeks off. Mind you, he thought you, not me, deserved it! He holds the RAF in such high regard that he will do almost anything to help the cause. His own son is in the RAF in a fighter squadron, so he was impressed to know you were a wireless operator in a bomber!'

'Of course I told him,' she said proudly when Ben raised his eyebrows as to how the senior partner of a firm of solicitors could have known this. 'Why not? I'm very proud of you.'

Ben gave her a lingering kiss and Olive, her arms round his neck, whispered in his ear. 'But the best news of all is that we are going to have a baby in September!'

'Are you sure? Are you absolutely certain?' Ben asked with rising excitement in his voice.

'Yes, absolutely, there's no doubt. The maternity wing at St Margaret's Hospital has confirmed it! All is well so far, except I'm having the most dreadful morning sickness. It isn't pleasant, but it goes after a while, and I'm quite prepared to suffer that. Isn't it exciting, Ben?'

Ben took her hand. 'I really wish that we could get married somehow. It would be our blessing to the baby. If there's anything we can do, we should try. It'd mean so much to both of us, let alone the child.'

'Ben, don't you think I've been wrestling with this for years? My church won't even consider a divorce, even if my husband consented. And now he's vanished or so it seems. There's no way I can contact him, even if I wanted to.

'Perhaps I could obtain a civil divorce, but it wouldn't be recognised by my church, and I don't want to be released from my religion. It would be like being excommunicated. I can't live with that, Ben. I do hope you understand. We have ourselves, and that's enough for me. I hope you feel this way too, although I know this will add to your problems with your family.'

'We won't let it spoil our great news, Olive. We've everything to look forward to. What does it matter whether or not we are legally married? We have ourselves and we'll manage.'

Ben put his arm around her and looked into the distance for a moment. Notwithstanding the excitement of the news, he knew that in the not-too-distant future he would have to confront this problem with his family. He knew they would be likely to disown him and his 'own' family of Olive and their child. It cast a shadow over his excitement at Olive's news, but he wouldn't allow his leave to be ruined by moments of painful difficulties over religious matters.

And nor did it do so. Ben attended Olive's next appointment at the maternity wing of St Margaret's. There, he learned that the obstetrician who would be dealing with her was none other than the Queen's obstetrician. *Well,* he thought, *that's a relief. I shan't have to worry about anything.*

He saw his mother on Sunday and arrived a few minutes before 12.30 p.m. Unusually, he was greeted with genuine warmth.

'How are you, Ben?' she asked and, sizing him up, continued, 'I can see they're feeding you! You've put on weight.'

'It's all that sitting in an aircraft. We don't get as much exercise as we used to.'

Florrie and Kitty were there. Both had changed out of uniform and were wearing similar utility floral dresses. Philip, Kitty's current boyfriend, sat next to her at the table. He had a cushy number as a corporal clerk in the War Office and, as he himself put it, seemed to be unlikely to see active service. Nevertheless, he seemed an all right guy, and Ben was happy for his sister.

Apparently, Florrie's boyfriend, who was also in the army, stationed at Aldershot, could not get a leave pass that weekend.

The lunch was pleasant and they left each other in a warm atmosphere of closeness, his mother even giving him a hug, telling him, 'Now, Ben, don't be silly, and you look after yourself.'

The leave, as it always did, went too fast. Ben and Olive visited baby shops and bought neutral colours. They discussed names for both a boy and girl. They laughed together and even discussed kindergartens and primary schools in the area.

'But Olive, all this may count for nothing. God willing, the war will soon be over and we'll be back in London. We may move out of the city centre. It would be better for the baby, and any others who may follow. We could live in the Tufnell Park area or Parliament Hill where there's some green space. We've got plenty of time to decide. Let's have the children first and then perhaps end the war!' he said, laughing.

Olive turned her face towards his and kissed him long and hard.

As he left the house at the end of his leave at 6.45 a.m. to return to his station by 1000 hours, he gave Olive a long and all-embracing hug.

'Olive, I'll phone you as often as I can. Expect calls at about 6 p.m. You must look after yourself now you're pregnant. Any problems, don't hesitate to go to the maternity wing. Don't tire yourself out and make sure you rest well.'

'And *you* must take good care of *yourself*, Ben. No heroics, keep safe and try to organise a leave pass to coincide with the birth, or at least shortly after. Don't forget the date. It's the first week in September, probably the third – the fourth anniversary of the outbreak of the war.'

Olive had promised she would not shed a tear at Ben's departure. She hadn't wanted him to see how anxious she was for him and now the family. She kept a large smile on her face, which he could remember her by.

Ben gave Olive a last, lingering kiss, picked up his bag and left for the railway station.

March 1943

When Ben reported to his station, the station warrant officer told him not to unpack but to gather all his kit as he was leaving at 1200 hours to be taken to the Number One Lancaster Finishing School at RAF Hemswell.

'You'll be flying Lancasters, Bloom. Much better than the

Halifax, so look sharp and report back at 1145. Time enough for you to get a snack in the canteen.'

At RAF Hemswell, Ben found himself billeted with the other sergeants at a place called Number Three Lancaster Green. The notices were all in Polish and, when Joe Black, the flight engineer, questioned this, he was told it had previously housed a Polish squadron but they had moved on.

The whole point of the conversion course was to get used to handling the Lancaster. Flight Sergeant George White, known as Chalky, introduced himself as the trainer. A man about five foot nine of stocky sturdiness, a broad face with a warm smile, and a head of short cropped hair more white than grey notwithstanding, he could have been in his mid-thirties. He wore ribbons, among which, Ben noticed, was the Distinguished Flying Medal.

'You'll be seeing a lot of me over the next two weeks. By then, you'll know everything there is to know about the Lancaster. Yes,' he had said, 'every bolt and screw and how to repair damage caused by flak. You'll be sent on to your Lancaster base sure in the knowledge that in combat you'll be the master of your craft. I always say that, if you look after your aircraft, it'll repay you by looking after you.'

Ben wondered how often he had made that little speech – presumably to each course that he had taken, and that must have been a good number.

Altogether, there were five crews, totalling thirty-five people, on the conversion course. They only needed to acquaint themselves with all the gadgetry, some of it new in design and application.

Ted Kingham, the pilot and the only officer among Ben's crew, handled the Lancaster well. He told the crew that a Lancaster was quite different to handling the Halifax, but that he considered it a much safer plane. This brought a cheer of relief from the crew. After a few bumpy landings, Ted found the line, and after that he was perfect. Ben, as usual, coordinated with the navigator, Bob Hutt, and all the crew practised their arts, with the turret gunners firing off their new up-to-date machine guns. They practised many times during the day over changing terrain, over the water at low level and at night. Towards the end of their tour, they were sent to a squadron for one day and night to check their proficiency for formation flying. They did not, however, go on operations.

The day before they completed their course, they heard some shocking news: Flight Sergeant Robinson and his crew had crashed on a training flight in their Halifax into a police station at Kirton in Lindsey, and all were dead. Ben had known Chuck Robinson at Doncaster, as well as many of his crew.

Because the crash had been in England and not caused by enemy guns, it seemed worse, somehow. *What a terrible waste of lives*, Ben thought. On returning from operations over France or Germany, losses were expected, and there were many. These, however, could be accepted as part of the war and everyone moved on. But a crash during training was something different and Ben's Lancaster crew, from which only a few had known Chuck and the others, all felt the loss heavily.

On the penultimate day of their course, the flight sergeant came up to Ben, took off his cap badge and handed it to him. 'Here you are, wireless operator. Pin this on your tie. You might get into trouble some day, and that's my good luck token for crews I've instructed. I've had two crews that have completed their thirty operational tours and they've both come back here and given me the cap badge back. I hope you'll do the same.'

'Sure I will,' said Ben. 'I'll be proud to wear it. It will keep me out of harm's way. I look forward to the day I can return it to you.'

'Sergeant Bloom, I know this is your second tour and so you know the ropes. You're a real glutton for punishment. I haven't had one yet who completed a double,' he said with a smile.

The crew of the Lancaster were posted to the operational station at RAF Waterbeach. Following the last flight at RAF Hemswell, and as they stood by their Lancs, waiting for the transport to take them to their mess, Ted Kingham thanked them all.

'I think, and those above us believe, we have the makings of a fine crew. I hope you'll all join me in the Lanc we'll be assigned to at Waterbeach. Hopefully we can remain as a crew. I'll be proud to be your skipper.'

Loud cheers and applause greeted him. 'Sure, Skip, we're all with you,' shouted his crew, almost in unison.

At RAF Waterbeach, Pilot Officer Ted Kingham was allocated Lancaster LL690J. Ted had organised a three-hour run in the Lanc the following morning and discussed the navigation with Bob Hutt. They cleared it with wing commander ops and took off at 0930 hours the following morning, having spent some time checking every part of the aircraft as they had been trained to do at RAF Hemswell. Joe Black, the engineer, mimicked their former training flight sergeant, Chalky White. 'Know every bolt and every screw in this plane before you fly,' he said in his deep Mancunian accent. They returned to Waterbeach at 1230 hours as arranged.

They then met with the large contingent of crews at the briefing meeting and had drinks with them in the mess. In the sergeants' mess, everyone – or everyone as far as Ben could see – drank pints of beer: Watney's Best. It was the staple diet and considerably cheaper than in the pubs. Ben didn't know whether there was tax on beer but certainly the RAF paid none, and the brewery was pleased to allow sales to servicemen at reduced prices.

They were now all members of 514 Squadron, which had an enviable record of operations. They'd be flying at night over Northern France, bombing aircraft and other armament factories, and then came the night-bombing of areas in Germany and the Ruhr, particularly the industrial towns of Duisburg, Essen and Wuppertal. Ben became very busy in exercising his ABC jamming the German transmitters and avoiding night-fighters. Ted was a skilled pilot, and somehow Ben and his colleagues felt safe with him. The more they flew on operations, the more they felt as if nothing could interfere with their success.

10

June 1943

'Sergeant Bloom, a moment, please.' The command came from the station warrant officer, probably the most important – and feared man – according to the NCOs and even some of the more junior officers. It was 0830 hours and Ben was just returning to the mess room, having breakfasted in the canteen.

Ben turned smartly and marched towards him, clattering to attention a yard away. One didn't walk when under command of the SWO.

'Bloom, I have been told that Captain Weitzman, the Jewish padre, will be coming to this station at 1000 hours this morning and wants to see all members of his faith. I have been told there are three at RAF Waterbeach, and you are to report to the adjutant's office at 0950 hours. Advise your colleagues where you are so that no one wastes time looking for you. Know where you ought to be at 1200 hours, although I somehow doubt Captain Weitzman will keep you that long. Is that clear, Sergeant Bloom?'

'Certainly, sir.'

At 0950 hours, Ben duly reported to the adjutant's office and the flight sergeant at reception took down his rank, number and name and sent him to into an adjoining waiting room.

Apart from the table and six chairs, the room was bare. Ben was joined shortly by AC2 Jack Gottlieb and SAC Leonard Goldman. Although they were not in his squadron, he'd met them both on the station. They had exchanged pleasantries mainly about where they lived and their respective Jewish communities. They'd not met for any religious services because there were only three and none of them were particularly observant.

Right on ten o'clock, the door swung open and Rabbi David Weitzman breezed in. Ben judged him to be in his late twenties, and he was wearing the most extraordinary uniform. It seemed to be nearly purple, with a white shirt and plain brown tie, and glistening brass buttons on his tunic. Ben noticed three pips on his shoulder flaps, denoting his rank of captain. He was clean shaven, which emphasised his youth, and he did not wear a dog collar, unlike most chaplains in the services.

The three of them stood to attention.

The rabbi took off his officer's cap and placed it on the table. He was wearing a small orange-coloured skull cap covering the crown of his head.

'Relax, everyone. Do sit down. I'm Rabbi David Weitzman, chaplain to the forces. Don't refer to me by rank. To you, I'm just rabbi. That's how you address me. No salutes unless you pass me on the parade ground. No "sirs", just plain rabbi. This is my first visit to RAF Waterbeach – army bases are my norm. So it's a pleasure to come here and meet the guys who are actually doing damage to the Nazis.

'Perhaps you haven't been told the information from Eastern Europe? Our people in the Baltic States, in Poland and Russia, are being slaughtered, and those who aren't killed immediately are being sent to concentration camps, where their life is brutal and short. They are rounding up Jews in France, Belgium and Holland and other occupied countries and even now in Germany and Austria. There's talk of mass executions and killings by gas, but it's not been officially confirmed. So, I have the utmost respect for you for risking your lives flying over enemy territory.

'Now, I'm here not to teach you Hebrew, nor necessarily to have a service. But if you wish to say a prayer with me, either in Hebrew or English, we can do so. You may find it a comfort. I have some booklets with me which I'll give to you. Now, introduce yourselves!'

Each of them did so, giving rank, name and number in a formal manner, despite the rabbi's clear preference for informality.

'I've come to hear what you've got to say,' he said, looking first at Leonard Goldman.

'I've no complaints. There's a bit of a choice – if we don't eat bacon, we can get some more beans. They're pretty good to us like that, and I haven't had any jibes or anti-Semitic comments.'

He looked at Jack Gottlieb, who said, 'I'm the same. When I first arrived, someone in my Section called me "an effing Yid", but the flight sergeant soon put an end to that.'

'That's good to hear,' the rabbi said. 'Here's my card for each of you. I don't know when I'll next be able to come again, but if you need me, the adjutant's office will contact me. On personnel matters, particularly religious, they are very good. They don't know how to deal with them so they "bless" me for taking this responsibility away from them. If there is, God forbid, a family death or major personal crisis, I can usually get compassionate leave for you. I might be able to get special leave, depending on operations, for the high festivals, but that might prove more difficult.

'We must realise that we live in difficult times. We must not be seen to complain or to seek preferential treatment. In my travels, I find that the authorities are generally cooperative where they can be. We Jews must fight and be seen to fight this war with all our strength.'

Ben nodded in agreement as if to confirm not only the thought but that the three of them were doing so.

The rabbi continued, 'Mental attitude is just as important as the physical. Remember, our people under Nazi rule are, in most cases, the elderly and children. They are certainly unarmed and non-combatant, and these defenceless people are being driven to their deaths because, like you, they are Jews. We're the privileged. We happen to have been born on the better side of the Channel. We are fighting on the right side with the right people as our allies.'

At this, Ben said, 'We don't disagree. This is why we're all here. This is my second tour – I had the right to withdraw after thirty ops. I'm not alone. I want you to know that there are many like me.'

Leonard and Jack nodded in agreement.

'Ben,' the rabbi replied, 'I know your RAF background and applaud it.'

He uttered a short prayer both in Hebrew and in English, to which they all said 'Amen'.

The rabbi looked at each of them with his intelligent eyes and asked, 'Now, do any of you want to talk to me privately? If you have a problem you wish to discuss with me in confidence, we can do so in the next room.'

He had spoken these last few words on a higher note, softly enquiring, not ordering. Ben admired his style, his youthfulness and his willingness to be of help. He had already made his decision.

Leonard and Jack looked at each other, and Jack said, 'No thanks, rabbi. All's well with us at the moment. We really appreciate your coming to the station to see us. If needs be, we'll contact you through the adjutant.'

Ben, who had been quiet throughout, said, 'Rabbi, if you could spare some of your time, I would like some advice in private.'

'Of course,' the young rabbi said. 'Certainly. Look, if Jack and you, Leonard, are finished here, I'll talk with Ben.'

At that, both Jack and Leonard stood, smiled their thanks and, despite the orders of the day, automatically saluted.

The rabbi did not return the salute but raised a hand in acknowledgement with the parting words to them, 'Let the Almighty be always with you and keep you safe.'

When the door had closed, the rabbi turned towards Ben. 'So, what would you like to talk to me about? Be as open as you can. Whatever you say will not leave this room without your knowledge and consent.'

There was a pause before Ben started. The rabbi noticed Ben pushing his hair back, a sure sign someone was suffering from some mental anguish.

'Take your time. I'm in no hurry. You can tell me all – the whole picture, please. I won't be embarrassed and nor should you be. I'll not be critical. I'm here to help.'

Ben went through his recent personal history: how and when he had met Olive; Olive's Catholic background; that her priest could give her no solace as to freeing her from the wreckage of her marriage; his enduring love, which was wholly reciprocated by Olive; the news of their soon-to-be-born child; the deception which Ben had found it necessary to carry out with his family, which he hated himself for doing but which he had yet to find an answer to; the difficult relationship he had with his mother.

All this poured out of Ben in a low, quiet and unassuming

voice without emotion. He told the rabbi about the strength of his relationship with Olive. He wished to remain in his family but thought his mother, once she knew the situation, would have nothing to do with him, Olive or the grandchild. Olive would like to be accepted and enveloped in a family life which she had never experienced. And even more, she wanted the child to be recognised and to be accepted.

The rabbi listened without interrupting. He made no notes. His expression remained warm, supportive and interested. He did not, as Ben knew some rabbis would, show annoyance, disapproval or even disgust at Ben's actions, which were contrary to orthodox faith. His face remained serene, his eyes always on Ben as if helping him to relate his story and to relieve him from some of the pain he was enduring. Ben came to the end simply by saying he had no ideas as to how and when he should tell his mother and his family of his true situation.

The rabbi paused. He was young, certainly intelligent, and Ben could see he was moved by the story he had just heard. Ben wondered if the rabbi had sufficient experience in life to guide him towards an acceptable path – towards a solution to this problem. *Well, now is the time*, Ben thought. *I'll soon find out.*

'Ben, you have told me a story both filled with love and sadness. I have several congregants who want to marry out of the faith, which causes distress to their families. In many cases, the problems within these families can be resolved once the heat and antagonism is taken out.

'Your case is the more serious because Olive is not in a position to marry. She is, as we in the orthodox faith well know, a sort of "chained" woman. Her absent husband cannot be found and apparently would be most uncooperative. Her church won't recognise such a divorce in any case.'

Ben nodded. 'That's our big problem.'

The rabbi continued, 'She apparently can't get a decree of nullity from her church, which is the reason she is "chained". If a nullity *could* be granted by her church, then she could, if she so wanted, marry you, legitimise the child and convert to Judaism, which would mean her children would be accepted in our faith. It would mean that a son could then have a *brit milah*. That's usually on the eighth day from his birth, in accordance with the biblical covenant with Abraham, of course, but there's no reason it couldn't be later.'

Ben must have looked slightly confused, as the rabbi smiled indulgently at him.

'It's not merely a circumcision. It is a deeply important spiritual ceremony with ancient prayers, admitting the child into the faith. It is a holy and spiritual occasion, not just a medical operation, and this can't take place if the child is not Jewish. In that case, only the medical aspect can take place, which has no meaning other than you prefer the child to have such an operation for health reasons. Since the religion can only derive from the mother, the fact you are Jewish is quite irrelevant. So you and Olive must decide what you both want in this relationship.'

'But what about my family?' Ben asked.

'I could help to bring *shalom* between you and your mother, whatever you and Olive decide on conversion. It won't be easy but it may soften the blow if you, Olive and I were to approach her together. She will then see that as a rabbi, I can particularly understand this kind of relationship in wartime. I could be the catalyst for a peaceful outcome. Why don't you both think about it?

'In the meantime, without breaking your or Olive's confidence, I should like to discuss it with my counterpart in the Catholic religion and see what we can achieve.'

Ben noted the rabbi's speech had been modulated at all times. He spoke slowly and deliberately, carefully choosing his words, which underlined the truth and sincerity of his speech. He seemed compassionate, and Ben thought he could not have placed his case with a more understanding man.

'I will make an appointment to see you hopefully within a month, Ben. I make no promises. It is not within my gift to help Olive, but I will do everything I can.

'If we can make progress, we can explore how you should tell your mother. I can understand she may react with some anger and even ferocity – I have witnessed such scenes myself.

'We Jews have long held traditions and customs, going back millennia to biblical times. It is ultimately a question of belief and loyalty ... respect, if you like, for the Fifth Commandment – "Honour your father and your mother".

'If you would like me to be present or even pay a visit on my own to your mother, I'd gladly do this. She may well understand in this terrible war, where you are in the front line of duty, risking your life every time you go on operations, and she might come to understand and accept her grandchild – and Olive.

'Think it over. I can't move without your consent. In the meantime, I shall see what may be achieved with the Romans, although I wouldn't place too much on that!'

Ben pondered for a brief moment on what the rabbi had said. 'You know, rabbi, I don't want to hurt your feelings, and I do respect what you say, but I feel rejected by my religion. I think of all the battles and wars in biblical days, the decimation of the Jews by the Crusaders on their way to the Holy Land, the Inquisition in Spain, the Hundred Years War and the Thirty Years War in Europe – and so many more around the globe all in the name of religion and beliefs. Not to mention the pogroms in the last few centuries in Russia and more recently in Poland, Germany and Austria. Is it worth it? If two reasonable human beings, Olive and me, merely want to get married, have children as we are doing and lead a loving and happy life, why should this be stopped in the name of religion?'

Ben sighed heavily. 'Sorry if I offend you, rabbi, but in my circumstances, I find it very difficult to understand. We are supposed to be fighting for a better world. And the present world is not being supportive or helpful in the circumstances that Olive and I find ourselves in.'

He pointed the silver chain round his neck with the emblem of the Magen David. 'You see here? My father gave me this to me on my thirteenth birthday on my bar mitzvah. It had belonged to his great grandfather in Lithuania in the early part of last century. He told me to always wear it. Despite orders to the contrary, flying over Germany and occupied territories, I wear it, rabbi. I wear it because I am a Jew and I don't care who knows it.'

The rabbi wove his fingers together. He was silent for a moment and then quietly replied, 'I know your pain well. You're not the only person in this predicament although, in my experience, yours is more difficult than most. I would be misleading you if I were to say it will all come right. Compromises can be made, and there might be little leeway to afford some kind of solution. But if there is not, then you and I must find a realistic path to tread. I promise you I'll see what I can do.

'I'll make a point of telling the adjutant I'll return to this station to see you. I can't say when at the moment, but it will be within a few weeks. I must discuss it with my colleagues in the Catholic Church and take further advice from the Beth Din – the House of Jewish Law – and from the liberal wing of our religion, which lends itself more readily to practical solutions.

'In the meantime, look after Olive and the child to come and more particularly yourself. Olive and your child will need you. Keep safe, and may the Almighty remain with you at all times.'

The rabbi concluded with a Jewish prayer in Hebrew and bestowed the priestly blessing on Ben.

They stood, shook hands and Ben left to return to his duties.

11

Early August 1943

The rabbi was true to his word. Four operations later, three over the Ruhr in Germany and one over Lyon in France to bomb an aircraft factory, Ben was told to report once again to the adjutant's office to meet with Captain Padre Weitzman.

Ben stood to attention when the padre arrived – in what Ben still considered a very curious uniform. The padre gave a welcoming smile, signed in the adjutant's visitors' book and ushered him into the same adjoining office where they had previously met.

'Well, I see the Lord is looking after you, Ben! We are together and that's what counts in today's world.'

'Sure, rabbi. Glad to see you. I hope you have good news.'

The rabbi smiled sadly. 'Not exactly, I'm afraid. I have spoken to a Roman Catholic priest. Without mentioning names, he's a person whom I know and respect. He has confirmed that a divorce would not be acceptable to his church. He also confirmed that Olive could apply for a nullity, but it would take years – particularly in wartime. The case would have to go to her priest, then on recommendation only to higher officers in the church, then again on recommendation to the papal nuncio and thence to the Vatican, and there it could be held up for considerable time in committees and be in a queue for applications from all over the world.

'In his experience, he said, he did not consider the chances of success were high. The Catholic procedures are detailed and complex, and he was reluctant to recommend that avenue. Of course, he suggested that you might convert to Catholicism, so the child, you and Olive would be accepted, albeit outside marriage. I didn't believe this would be a satisfactory solution to you, though.'

Ben nodded his agreement.

'An alternative solution would be for Olive to apply for a civil divorce based on three years' desertion by her husband. In that case, you could marry, legitimise your child and then, if Olive agreed to convert to Judaism, which I could arrange, the child would be accepted in the Jewish religion, conferring all the rights and benefits as to the upbringing of a Jewish child.

'That is the best offer on the table. Discuss it with Olive. If you want me to be with you both, I shall be pleased to do so. You know I'm very willing to meet with your mother. It might help.'

Ben sighed. Being a wireless operator in a Lancaster Bomber was worrying in itself. The continual drain on his nervous system with night-flying, facing heavy flak, seeing neighbouring Lancasters being hit and falling like uncontrolled leaves in flames to the ground without any parachutes opening, losing friends – the guys he drank with in the mess and in the adjoining country pubs – it was all beginning to overwhelm him. The occasional weekend lunches with his mother and family were becoming fewer and fewer as he sought thirty-six-or forty-eight-hour leave passes to be with Olive.

'I'll speak to Olive,' he said. 'You've set out the only constructive steps ahead very clearly. But she was brought up latterly in her youth in a convent. It may prove difficult for her. It seems, as she once said to me, we just have different gods. I know I shouldn't be thinking this, particularly after all your words and advice. But what with this war, the continuous deaths of my friends and colleagues, the deaths of those we never see or hear about from our bombing raids for which we are responsible, what relevance is religion in today's world? What does it matter, rabbi, whether you or I are Jewish, Christian or Muslim?

'So far as I'm concerned, and with my experiences from the Battle of Cable Street against the fascists and in this war, and my hopeless situation with my family, it seems I have only religion to blame. So what can you say in the name of religion to Sergeant Ben Bloom, serving in His Majesty's Royal Air Force?'

Before the rabbi could answer, Ben added, 'All I want is a life with Olive and my child – with the woman I love and whom I know loves me. I don't want to have to face a more aggressive war with my mother and family based on religion.'

The rabbi nodded slowly. 'I have no ready or glib answer for you. It's ultimately a matter of faith – what you and your ancestors kept throughout the centuries of oppression, from the time of the exodus from Egypt. We have always lived in tragic periods of history, but we never succumbed. As a religion, we retained our faith, just as we did when you were fifteen at the Battle of Cable Street. Nothing has changed from that. And that's why I am here to give you support. I can speak with Olive. I can speak to your mother and your brother and sisters. You should not stand alone. You're a serving airman, Ben. Use me when you require.'

Ben, resignation in his voice, concluded the interview by saying, 'I'll relay all you have said to Olive and see where we go from there. I want you to know that, despite my frustrations at this religious divide, I really am grateful for your time and interest in my affairs, rabbi.'

'Well, that's exactly why I'm here. It'll help me to know that your problems can be resolved. Please keep me informed and if you'd like me to do anything, just let me know.'

Several days later, in mid-August, Ben was home with Olive on a weekend leave pass. She was now eight months pregnant. She looked large in her maternity dress and her face had, in Ben's view, broadened. She looked happy and serene, and she was pleased with her condition – even excited in her anticipation of the birth.

When Ben had showered and changed, he recounted all that he had discussed with the padre. Olive listened quietly then, when he was finished, said, 'Ben, you know I fully respect what your rabbi advises. But for me to convert to Judaism for the benefit of the family is not a principle I can agree with. It would be selfish. It would only be for the comfort of our outside family – for your mother, brother and sisters. I'm not even sure my conversion would satisfy them. In my mind and in my conscience, I know it would be wrong. I have nothing against Judaism – I respect it as an old and good religion, but it is not *my* religion and never really be. I would always feel an outcast.'

She took Ben's hand in her own. 'We have each other. Soon we'll have our baby – and hopefully more after that. Why do we need to consider religion as if it were a political party to join to pay our dues? Even if others don't accept us, we'll survive and live happily together. And it will be an even greater incentive to ensure our lives remain entwined.

'We could visit your mother and take our baby – her first grandchild – to her to explain our love for each other. To show during this terrible war that the gods cannot divide us and that love and humanity ride above the storms. If she rejects us, at least we know where we stand, although we'll never give up trying to reconcile the differences. Time is a great healer. We don't have to change the rules to suit our lives. I don't want to turn my back on my beliefs to resolve a problem which really shouldn't exist.'

Ben listened to Olive's argument without interruption. He couldn't pretend that, although her conversion might – and only *might* – resolve his family's problems, it wasn't guaranteed to do so. Of course it would help, but would it be a solution? He could not promise that.

Ben was tired. His shoulders were dropping, and his arms and hands were listless. His growing weariness was evidenced by his paleness. He was fatigued from the continual sapping of his strength from the anxieties of flying over enemy territory. The bomber losses were increasing to unacceptable levels, and he knew his 'luck' could not last forever. He couldn't fight on all fronts. Olive meant everything to him, and he wasn't prepared to press her into an unwilling position.

So what? he thought. When the crunch came, he, Olive and the child would survive. If others in his family rejected them, so be it. He had tried. He could not resolve the problem. He would move on.

Kivi was born on 1 September 1943, at St Margaret's Hospital, Epping, with the Queen's obstetrician in attendance. The news was relayed to Ben who, as the wireless operator of his Lancaster, was the first to hear from the operations room a half hour before they landed at RAF Waterbeach. The intercom of the Lancaster LL690J was loud with congratulations.

'Drinks all round, post briefing!' said the skipper.

12

16 June 1944

It was just after 7.15 p.m. on the evening of 16 June. Olive had fed Kivi and put him in his cot, tucked up with his favourite teddy bear. She was about to prepare supper for herself when she heard the phone. She was tired. The last ten days had been trying; Kivi was beginning to teethe and his crying required her to soothe his gums and rock him gently to sleep. She had had a number of disturbed nights which, with her daily work routine, had taken their toll.

It wasn't only Kivi. She had placed him in Mrs Robinson's crèche in the morning, went to feed him during lunch hour and had returned to her work at the solicitor's office before collecting Kivi at 5.50 p.m. She was tired, and not only due to looking after Kivi but also because she was five months pregnant with their second child. She reached the phone on its fifth ring.

The voice on the phone was not Ben. It was hesitant and polite. 'Is that Olive?'

'Yes, who's speaking?'

'I'm Harry Garton.' There was a pause. 'A good friend of Ben's.' There was another pause.

Olive sensed it was not a good call. *Who was Harry Garton? Why is he calling?* Questions flashed through her mind. *Where is Ben?*

'I'm afraid I've got some bad news,' Harry went on. 'Ben's plane didn't return to base earlier this morning. It should have arrived at three in the morning latest. I'm afraid there's no news. They may have bailed out. We just don't know.'

There was a silence. Olive could not take it in. She had always known she might get a call like this. She had imagined what would be said and how she might react. But now she realised she was living in the present. This was no make-believe. This was the real thing, and she was paralysed with fear. She knew that all those who flew on bombing missions might not come back. But this would not happen to Ben. *Not to Ben.*

She began to sob.

Harry paused. Eventually, he heard himself say, 'Olive, the adjutant asked me to call you. Notice of being missing in action is sent only to next of kin. Officially, this was recorded as his mother and not you, but Ben often spoke of you. He left me an envelope with a letter telling me what to do if he did not return from an operation. I waited till now in the hope we would hear some news of him, but there hasn't been any.'

Harry could hear Olive sobbing and wasn't sure what more he could say.

'Look, if we hear anything at all, I'll call you, good or bad. In the meantime, we all have faith here that he and his crew may be prisoners of war. We should hear from the International Red Cross – they're given names by both sides of who has been taken prisoner or died. I promise to keep in touch.'

Olive couldn't reply, and her sobs grew louder. Harry ended the call by saying he would call again later in the week.

She slumped onto the settee. She could not restrain the flood of tears that was cascading down her cheeks.

'Oh, Ben. Ben, where are you? Please, please be safe. Come back to me,' she cried.

She could not eat the supper she had prepared. She

wanted to take a sleeping pill but felt she should not during her pregnancy. But she knew she had to remain strong for Kivi's sake.

The following day, Olive took Kivi to Mrs Robinson's crèche with his prepared milk and lunch before walking on to the solicitor's office. She did not mention her news to her colleagues. She tried to hide her feelings, because she knew that, once she mentioned it, everyone would try to comfort her, and she was just not up to take that on. Ben must be alive, perhaps hidden in a French farmhouse waiting for the time to return. She held on to this belief. They had their lives to live together. There was much more to achieve.

Just after 5.30pm, before collecting Kivi, she paid a visit to the Roman Catholic Church of St Mary's and knelt and prayed. She paid for, and placed, a candle, which she lit close to the altar.

'This is for you, Ben. You are alive and well and you *will* return.' The light in the candle flickered for a moment and then settled.

As she wheeled Kivi in his buggy back to their home, she realised this had been her first visit to church since before she had met Ben. She felt the better for having gone. Her visit, the lighting of the candle, had been a source of comfort.

The next few days were surreal. Olive went through the motions of living as if in a trance. Kivi kept her busy and took her mind back to the basics. Clutching hold of him, washing him, feeding him, cuddling him, loving him and dressing him, her days were the same: crèche, office, crèche and home.

Six days after Harry Garton had broken the news, he phoned again in the evening.

'What news, Harry? Give me only good news,' she pleaded.

'Not altogether, Olive. There may be some hope, however. We now know that Ben's Lancaster came down shortly after midnight on 16 June, close to the small French town of Iwuy. Six bodies were found and identified. Five were buried in the cemetery in the nearby town of Rieux by the French under German supervision. A Lancaster has a crew of seven, though, and Ben's body was not found.

'The sixth body was that of Sergeant Bob Hutt. He was found a few miles away and was buried at Iwuy. It was thought he had been blown out of the plane. So we all live in hope that Ben survived and is hiding. He may have been able to bail out. We just don't know.

'I also have a message from the adjutant. He would have spoken to you himself but thought it better coming from me. It's not good news, but the adjutant thought you ought to know.

'If Ben is found to have died, the RAF pension and state pension can only go to the next of kin who is, as you know, his mother. There's no provision to make any payments to you. I know this will come as an added blow, but the adjutant thought you ought to be aware of your situation in that event. You should get more information on this. As you work in a solicitor's office, you should be able to get first-class advice and see who else might be able to assist.

'The adjutant also told me that, should you wish to meet or speak with him on the telephone at RAF Waterbeach, he would be most pleased to do so. Ben is held in the highest esteem here.'

Olive held herself in and kept herself from crying.

'I greatly appreciate your calling, Harry. Had it not been for you and your friendship with Ben, I should still be waiting for his call or a visit on one of his leave passes. Sure,

I shall take advice as you suggest. And if I need to speak with the adjutant, I shall call him. I have the RAF Waterbeach number.

'I still have hope, Harry. I feel Ben is alive. They can't find his body, so he's around. If you hear anything further, please do ring, good or bad. I appreciate your help. Do I get an official letter or telegram from the War Office or station commander? As it is, I know nothing other than what you've told me.'

'No, Olive. I'm afraid not. The rules state only the next of kin are advised. That seems to be his mother. You may wish to contact her.'

'Thanks, Harry. I'll handle it. Goodbye.'

Olive paused by the phone, trying to collect her thoughts. Should she contact Ben's mother? This could be the opportunity to introduce her to her grandchild. It would come as a shock, but it might just mitigate her loss a little. But Olive was aware of Ben's deception over the years and wasn't sure how to deal with that. At the very worst, though, his mother could only throw her out, and then she would at least know where she stood. But, with the birth of her next child approaching, she realised she would not be able to continue working and would need financial help to care for herself and two young children.

On the following Sunday, at just after ten thirty in the morning, there was a knock on the door. An officer in a purple-coloured uniform saluted her and introduced himself.

'I'm Rabbi Captain David Weitzman, a Jewish chaplain to the forces. I met Ben on two occasions at RAF Waterbeach. I'm aware he's currently missing in action, and I hope you'll allow me to talk with you.'

He was young, kindly and warmly respectful. Olive

noticed the three pips on his epaulettes. 'Come in, captain. I'm just making a cup of tea. My young son is crawling about with his toys in the living room. We don't have a nursery except where he sleeps.'

'Wonderful. I could do with a cup of tea. No milk or sugar please, and do call me rabbi or padre if you prefer. We are not rank-conscious in this calling,' he said with a smile.

When they had sat down on the settee and, after he had been introduced to Kivi who, on seeing a new face, had smiled and gurgled at him, David Weitzman started the conversation.

'Olive, you may not know that I met with Ben on two occasions at RAF Waterbeach. It's part of my duties to meet with all those of my faith and see what I can do to help, if they require any. I formed a good impression of Ben. He told me both your histories.

'I know you and Ben could never get married because you couldn't get a divorce or nullity from your church. I'm aware that you do not wish to convert to Judaism, and I am not here to put you under any pressure to do so. I pray for Ben's safe return, as you do. But, in the meantime, I have been advised by the adjutant of RAF Waterbeach that no payments can be made to you – only to Ben's mother as his next of kin.

'I also know, as Ben told me, that he had never mentioned you to his mother and had, as he had stated, deceived his mother in seeing her and his family at her house for occasional Friday evenings when he was on leave. So his mother, I presume, knows nothing of you and Kivi, or your current pregnancy. I had offered to help break the news to her to try to bring peace between them and you but he had not authorised me to do so, although he *was* thinking about it.

'So, first things first. How will you be able to look after yourself and the children when presumably you will not be able to work? Secondly, can we make plans for you to meet with Ben's mother? It may not be a pleasant occasion and, as I said to Ben, I would be very happy to be present with you. Alternatively, I could arrange to meet with her first to break the news of you and the children. I shall take my orders from you, Olive.'

Olive had listened in respectful silence, carefully weighing his words.

'Frankly, rabbi, I have no idea what I can do for money once I leave work. I had thought of placing myself, however distasteful that is to me, on his mother's charity. I have no idea how she might react to my meeting her, though. She may well throw me, out but sooner or later I must try. I thought I should wait until our second child is born and then present them to their grandmother. She may feel it right to help.'

'That's good thinking. Sooner rather than later, you'll certainly have to meet Mrs Bloom. Let me know if you want any help from me. I certainly don't want to pressure you, only to help as you may want.

'Now, I should tell you about the assistance you might get through the RAF. I've written down all these authorities and addresses for you, and I suggest you write and tell them all the facts. Some of these associations may be able to assist you and the children and help out with school fees in the future. It'll pay to keep in touch with them. They are bound to send someone to discuss your situation.

'First, there is SSAFA – the Soldiers, Sailors, Airmen and Family Association. They may be your best contact. Secondly, the RAF Widows' Association. You may not qualify since you are not technically a widow and they tend to be very particular as to their rules, but it's certainly worth a letter or two.

'Then there is the RAF Families Federation. There are two organisations involved in the search for those missing in action: the International Red Cross and MRES, the Missing Research Enquiry Service. This has just been set up, and they expect it will be active for a short time – perhaps five or seven years after the end of the war. You should try all of them. One or more may just be able to help you either financially or in your search for Ben. A lot depends on luck but, as they say, Olive, if you don't buy a lottery ticket, you won't win.'

'Thanks, rabbi. This is all so helpful,' Olive said, touching the addresses on the piece of paper he'd handed her. 'If there's any chance of finding any information about Ben, I'll seek it out however long it takes. He may be still alive. He may be found and, even at the worst, if he is dead, he'll need a decent burial and a place where I can go with our children and be with his spirit.'

Rabbi Weitzman nodded and added, 'In the meantime, I might have a possible solution for your immediate financial problems. Can you leave this to me, Olive? I know a number of people who might be able to arrange assistance, one in particular by the name of Herschel Glazer, if I can get hold of him. He's a quiet and unusual chap who asks no questions and would look after you and the children. He works for a private charity funded by wealthy benefactors. I'll get in touch with him and, if he contacts you, they'll mention my name so you'll know that they are kosher – proper people who you can trust.

'I know you'll have many problems without Ben at present, and I'm here to help. I hope you'll accept my suggestions so I can make some calls on your behalf.'

'Rabbi, I know Kivi and my unborn child are not of your faith, but I don't want to decline your generous offer. I'm in despair. At this moment, I can't see a future. I'll accept anything you can do with great gratitude. It's more than kind of you to think of assisting me. Your presence here today is, to say the least, a miracle. I've not known where to turn and you appear to me this morning as a saviour.'

The rabbi took this as a compliment, although not certain that he liked the parable of being a 'saviour' – it was a little too Catholic for him.

'You'll hear soon from either me or someone on my behalf. Here's my card. Please call me when you want. I'll keep in touch with you, and I wish you every blessing for your forthcoming happy event.'

13

5 July 1944

Herschel Glazer was a small man, perhaps five foot four inches if you counted his high-heeled boots, which had seen better days. Olive noticed that his suit jacket cuffs were fraying at the edges. In his quaint manner of speech with a foreign accent, he had introduced himself to Olive over the telephone and had made it clear he had been well advised by Rabbi Weitzman on her problem. He told her he had taken the liberty of making appropriate enquiries with his own people and was now able – with her consent – to make decisions, which could be implemented immediately or within days. As with the rabbi, he wore a small skull cover over the crown of his head, which he kept in place with a woman's hair clip attached to the small area of hair on his mostly balding head.

Unlike the rabbi, though, he was a busy person, seemingly always on the move even when he was sitting. He had waved away a cup of tea offered by Olive. But the directed warmth of his personality towards Olive, his client for the moment, was unmistakable. He was there to please and wanted nothing in return.

'I want you to move to South Woodford as soon as possible,' he told her. 'We have a nice and clean flat on the ground floor for you, perhaps a little larger than this. It has two bedrooms. It's very close to a park so, when the children grow a little, they'll have a place to play. Usual additions: a bathroom with toilet and wash basin in good condition, a kitchen with all mod cons and even a coat cupboard close to the front door with extra space for your cases. Look, here are some photographs.'

Herschel rummaged in his jacket and, after checking three of his pockets, found what he was looking for in the fourth.

'Also, there's a communal garden with lawn at the rear. There are only three flats so, in the summer months, you can lie out there with rugs and enjoy an element of privacy. It's fully furnished, even with pots and pans, cutlery and crockery, all, I may say, in clean condition.

'And the beauty of this arrangement, Olive, is that you pay no rent or rates! No outgoings at all. On top of this, we'll pay you ten pounds a week. It'll go automatically into your bank account so you should have no monetary worries.

'You should be safe in South Woodford. There has been no bombing in the area so you should be free from air attacks.'

Olive, who was never open-mouthed, had to work hard to maintain her calmness in the face of this munificence being thrown at her.

'Herschel, all this is magnificent and resolves all my problems! I couldn't have thought this could happen in my lifetime. Tell me, who is my fairy godfather? And why should they or he be so helpful to me?'

Herschel waved a hand dismissively. 'Easy answers, Olive. First, we have wealthy benefactors who buy these properties not for income but for capital growth. They are aware the war is near to an end. After the war, with our returning troops and what with all the bomb damage and loss of houses, everyone will require housing. Property values will increase substantially. They are not in need of income as that complicates their tax returns. So they look to me to provide them with good, well-deserving tenants, like you.'

'Well, I can understand their logic,' said Olive. 'So I just happen to be the fortunate beneficiary of their largesse. But even so, why should they pay me a monthly sum?'

'Well, these people are Jewish and came from Germany and Austria shortly before the war. They feel privileged in assisting you with a husband who fought and, please God, may survive this war. They are very conscious they owe their freedom and life to people like Ben. Ben fought the war, but they could not do so because they are considered "friendly enemy aliens" and for the most part are too old for active service. They are fine people and naturally charitable. They see you as a most deserving case, particularly on the recommendation of Rabbi David Weitzman.

'Also, Ben fought in the Battle of Cable Street in 1936 as a boy, and this in itself is enough of a credential for my people to be thankful for his life. They pray fervently for his safe return after this war has ended.'

Olive gave a sigh of thanks and pleasure. She realised she would have to live off charity for some time ahead as there was no other foreseeable support. She would not be able to work for several months, and it would take time to settle herself with her new baby and with Kivi.

'Herschel, I want you to tell my supporters how grateful I am. If they wish to visit me and the family, they'll always be most welcome. Also, please tell them that, as soon as I can organise myself, I shall ask them to cease payments to me. I want them to know that it is not my intention to live off their charity any longer than I need. As soon as I can organise myself with work, I'll let you know. Let me have your address and telephone number.'

'Here's my card. Can I take it that, let's say Friday week, I can bring a van to clear your furniture and your goods and take you and Kivi to your new home? You must give notice to your landlord of your departure and, please, make sure you have paid all bills to the date you leave. I'll call for you both at eleven in the morning. You'll hopefully be in your new home before 1 p.m. May I suggest you get a recommendation from your doctor or maternity nurse for the replacement in South Woodford? You ought to check in with her within days of your arrival. Get that fixed while you are still here.'

'Thanks, Herschel, I'll do that.'

And as Herschel was leaving, he added, 'And don't forget to keep a copy of your notice to your landlord. Send it to him today!' And with that, he was gone, moving quickly on his short stubby legs to his car.

Olive felt euphoric. This was the best news she'd received in a long time. She felt secure now and, for the first time since Harry had first telephoned, she felt that the burden of looking after Kivi and the forthcoming baby had been lifted. She danced a few steps around the room to express her relief in her changing circumstances but quickly realised she needed to sort herself in readiness for the move.

She began to methodically pack all her clothes and those of Ben's into the cases they had always used. She made lists of all other household chattels she needed to take with her and placed them in a corner of the living room.

Packing Kivi's clothes and toys would take no time, so she left these for the morning of the move.

She prepared the notice to the landlord and dutifully kept a copy before sending it in the post. She called in to her old firm to say goodbye and thank them for their many kindnesses. She told them she was moving to be with friends in South Woodford. She cleared herself with her doctor and maternity nurse and obtained names and telephone numbers of corresponding services in South Woodford. The doctor gave Olive a letter of introduction and details of her medical record. All was set for the move.

On time at 11 a.m. on Friday, 14 July 1944, the van arrived – without Herschel but with an easy-going cockney driver. Having introduced himself to Olive, Bert took the luggage down to the van, refusing to allow her lift anything in her clearly late state of pregnancy. He carried Kivi and handed him to Olive, who stepped into the rear two seats.

Bert cheerily began to drive to South Woodford. Fortunately for Olive, he didn't engage her in conversation but regaled her with the excitements in his own life of taking servicemen wounded in recent battles in Italy to their homes from their hospitals or places they had been sent to recuperate after operations. He himself came from Barking in Essex. He talked non-stop until almost at the address in South Woodford, when he asked Olive where she had come from. Olive managed to change the subject and told him how much she was looking forward to being in her new home.

On arrival, he presented her with the keys of the flat and carried all her worldly chattels into her living room.

'Good luck in yer new home and also with yer new baby. Hope all goes well, Olive,' he called as he turned towards his van.

It didn't take her long to unpack and store her few belongings. She made Kivi a lunch of shredded lettuce and baked beans. She was relieved to see the flat in such clean condition, which Herschel had predicted. She had noted the park with its swings and slide on the opposite side of the road, within a hundred yards of her flat. Also adjacent to the park were some useful small grocery and repair shops. All seemed to be very convenient.

She was pleased, excited and happy to be in her new home. She felt as if an enormous weight had been taken off her shoulders. At least she now had a larger, brighter home. She would concentrate on Kivi and the new baby when he or she arrived. She wanted Ben to approve and be proud of her and the children. She vowed to bring them up with love and remembrance of their father. Despite these maudlin thoughts, she was intent in keeping Ben alive in her mind. *He will return. He will be found*, she reminded herself.

She put Kivi in the buggy and wheeled him out to explore the surrounding area.

14

7 November 1944

Despite Herschel's confident assertion that South Woodford was free from air raids, from early June the south of England and particularly the London area was being incessantly bombed by V1 – and later V2 – rockets, causing considerable damage and distress. Three houses in a street two away from Olive's were hit and a mother and two young children were killed. A week later, two adjoining shops at the end of the High Street were destroyed but fortunately it was a Wednesday afternoon and they had been closed.

At the moment of birth, with the midwife present, the noise from the ack-ack guns firing at the V1 rockets in the adjacent park and the nearby explosions were causing panic. The mood wasn't helped by Kivi screaming in his cot at the side of Olive's bed. The lamp, which had been propped up at the top of the bed, fell on Olive. She had been in labour for more than eight hours. The baby was large, and Olive had haemorrhaged. The midwife called the doctor and took the newborn baby to a couple she knew in the next street, saying Olive was too weak to nurse him. Olive had intended to call the baby Paul if it were a boy, so Paul he became.

When they had all gone, Olive found enough strength to rise from her bed and, putting a coat on over her nightie, hurried to the house to get her baby back. She had left Kivi alone and asleep in his cot. She thanked her neighbour – Jane Perkins – profoundly for having taken in Paul and insisted she was well enough to have her baby returned. Jane carried Paul in his shawl and helped Olive settle him in his carry cot back in her home. Then Olive was left alone with her two children.

The house had not quite been the paradise described so wonderfully well by the excitable and enthusiastic Herschel. All requirements for the new baby, including stacks of nappies, were neatly piled in a cardboard box in the bathroom. Kivi's clothes were on wire hangers on the hook on the back of his bedroom door, and Olive's winter clothing was packed in a case under her bed. Space was very tight.

Nevertheless, she had much to be pleased about. Her rent was free. She was being given a stipend from the charity, without which she could not have managed at all. She was at least independent and, although life, as she envisaged the next few months, would be hard, somehow she would manage.

She had no family to depend upon or anyone, really, to give her succour. The neighbours were kind and helpful, particularly Jane, who kept a close watch on Olive and the boys. Over the next few weeks, several had dropped in to see whether they could take Kivi out in his buggy, giving some respite.

A few days after Paul had arrived, a large envelope with a congratulations card perked her up, but what really helped was a sizeable cheque for fifty pounds for her and the two children. This had come from her charitable supporters, whom she had never met. She did not have their address to thank them, but she did have Herschel's telephone number and the flat had a telephone. So she called Herschel and wept her thanks over the phone.

Harry Garton hadn't telephoned for some time, and she knew that, if he had had any news, good or bad, he would have called. However, she could not remain silent and telephoned RAF Waterbeach. When the operator said they could not contact Sergeant Garton, she asked to speak to the adjutant's office. When she gave her name as Sergeant Bloom's wife, the adjutant took the call.

'No Olive – I hope you don't mind me calling you Olive – there hasn't been any news of Ben. We have pressed the International Red Cross, and they made enquires on the German side, but they had nothing to report. In a way, that leaves the door open for Ben's return. The Allies are advancing through France and may pick him up. He may be in a camp in Germany without his papers or memory, which is why perhaps the Germans have no details of him.'

Olive read out Ben's mother's address and telephone number from the book in which Ben had written them.

'Yes, I can confirm from our details that his mother lives in Brondesbury Park and, yes, that is her telephone number.'

'Thank you, sir,' she answered.

'Do please keep in touch, Olive. We shall of course tell you immediately if we hear any news.'

She quietly put down her phone.

Olive knew in her heart that the time had come to face Ben's mother. How could she put it off any further? She had two sons by Ben. His mother presumably had no idea and must be mourning her son, just as Olive was. She needed more resources and certainly could not ask her 'sponsors'. She could not work yet as she could not leave Paul in a crèche at so tender an age, just a few weeks old. If Ben's mother could show some support for the children for a year or so, she thought she could find a job and would then be able to manage.

She took a deep breath, calmed herself and called the number. The sound of the call ringing seemed to take forever. As it rang, three, four, five times, she almost felt relieved that

Ben's mother might not be in. And then the phone was picked up.

'Yes, who is it?' came the enquiring voice of an elderly woman.

Olive's heart sank. The voice sounded impatient, rasping and unwelcoming. She took a deep breath.

'I'm Olive, Mrs Bloom—'

'How do you know my name?' she interrupted.

'You're Ben's mother. He's told me so much about you.'

Olive heard a gasp at the other end of the phone. 'Ben's missing. He's never spoken to me about you. Who are you?'

Olive willed herself to stay calm. 'We've not yet met, but I've heard so much about you from Ben. You're not aware that Ben and I were living together, and in view of his being missing in action, I thought it right to call you and hopefully we could meet.'

There was silence at the other end of the phone.

Olive persisted. 'If you don't mind, perhaps I could call on you at a more convenient time? I could explain the past and why Ben felt he couldn't tell his family of our union.'

Olive paused, hoping that Ben's mother would at least say something comforting. She heard instead a cold, uninviting voice.

'So *you're* Olive. The only reason I've heard of you is because Ben's RAF station sent me all his personal belongings as I'm his next of kin. I saw your letters to Ben and photographs. It came as a great shock. He could have introduced you to me. If you weren't married, why do you want to see me? I have nothing to say to you.'

'I understand your feelings, Mrs Bloom, but I wouldn't be ringing unless I thought I owed a duty to you to tell you that you have two grandchildren – Kivi, now sixteen months, and Paul, who was born after Ben went missing in June. I thought you should know and would like to see them. They're part of your family, and you have a right to know and see them.'

There was a long pause, so long that Olive found herself asking, 'Are you there, Mrs Bloom? Did you hear what I said?'

'I heard what you said, but I don't like what I heard. I really don't want to meet you, but if, as you say, the children are Ben's, then perhaps you ought to show them to me. I'll be home next Tuesday at 11 a.m. Presumably since you phoned, you have my address. You had better bring the birth certificates to show me the children are Ben's.'

'Thank you, Mrs Bloom. I'll be with you next Tuesday,' Olive said, but Ben's mother had already put her phone down.

Olive had prepared herself for this ordeal – for ordeal it had been. She knew she could not put off the meeting any longer. If she did, she knew Ben's mother would be able to hold that against her as if she were trying to hide her grandchildren from her, so it was imperative for her to open the dialogue. She was, in any event, in great need of support, financial more than moral, although the latter would be a comfort if she and the boys were to be accepted by the family. They'd been living off cheap food. The costs of the baby's requirements were constant and expensive. Olive kept her own expenses to the absolute minimum; she kept the heating as low as possible, wearing an extra cardigan when necessary and doubling up with clothes for the boys.

She thought she could ask Ben's mother for assistance – not for her, as she realised that would not be forthcoming, but at least for the two grandchildren. She was in despair in trying to make ends meet each week. The money from her benefactors was continuing but, although it was enough to pay for the clothes required for the boys and general expenses, it did not cover the food bills each week. She certainly couldn't ask for an increase to her 'gifted payments'. She was grateful for what she received, but she had no one she could turn to for help other than the possibility of Ben's mother supporting her grandchildren.

So, on Tuesday, 14 November, Olive, holding Kivi and with Paul in a lightweight pram, caught the bus to Golders Green and then changed to take them to Brondesbury Park. From there, it wouldn't be more than a quarter of a mile to Ben's mother's house. Although it was cold, it was a crisp dry day, so she didn't arrive in falling rain.

She ensured Kivi was dressed as smartly as possible: neat, short trousers, white open necked shirt, navy pullover under a coat which, although second hand, fitted him well. Paul was warmly tucked up in his swaddling clothes.

Olive rang the bell just a minute or so after 11 a.m. She waited patiently for at least two minutes before she heard someone come down the hallway to open the door. She reflected that two minutes in such circumstances seemed like an hour. Thoughts of her 'welcome' swirled around her mind. She swallowed hard and promised herself that no matter what insults or language she might encounter, she would be the 'lady' and remain calm under any flak that might be thrown at her. She would endeavour to reason with Mrs Bloom for the boys, not for herself.

She turned to Kivi, waiting patiently with her on the doorstep. 'Now be good, Kivi. You're going to meet someone very special.' Kivi nodded.

The door opened and the woman in front of her was

neither smiling nor welcoming. She was shortish, as Ben had been, with grey hair and wearing a non-descript woollen calf-length black dress and a black cardigan with a dark red imprint of flowers. Having looked Olive up and down over several seconds, in a flat voice without a hint of warmth she stated rather than asked, 'I suppose you're Olive and these are my supposed grandchildren. Well, you'd better come in.'

It was a large detached house with high ceilings, and Olive presumed it had probably been built in the late Victorian period. She and the children were led down the hallway into a large reception room, which Mrs Bloom referred to as her lounge.

There was a large standing bookcase along the wall, complete with hardbacked books which clearly had been read over the years. There were a number of family photographs on a small table showing Mrs Bloom and her husband, one with Ben and his younger brother and one with his three sisters in their young teens. And one of the family of seven. Olive noted that no refreshments were offered. She didn't need any but she thought it would have been an ice-breaker and a normal act of hospitality to lighten the atmosphere of what clearly was to be a difficult meeting for them all.

There were two men sitting in comfortable sofas who immediately stood on their entry. Mrs Bloom, in a perfunctory manner, said by way of introduction, 'Gentlemen, this is Olive Bell and her two children.'

She then sat herself down on the settee, leaving the third sofa for Olive.

Olive settled Kivi on the floor with two toys she had brought with her and placed the lightweight pram with the sleeping Paul just inside the door. As she took her seat on the remaining sofa, the elderly gentleman introduced himself.

He looked to be in his late seventies. Bowed with a rounded back, he could not have been more than five foot six. His thin hair was clearly disappearing.

He spoke slowly. 'I'm Tanzer Phillips. I was originally in partnership with Mr Bloom when we first set up the factory at Hackney Marshes in 1902. I moved on from the business a number of years later and have remained close friends with Mrs Bloom and the late Mr Bloom ever since.

'Mrs Bloom thought I should be here for this meeting and I believe, in all the circumstances, you will understand she did not want to see you alone.'

He gave a short nod before returning a few steps to take his seat.

The other gentleman stretched out his hand, which Olive took to shake as he presented himself to her. He was in his mid-forties. He wore a well-fitting formal dark suit with a white shirt and modest-coloured tie.

'I'm Adam Rose and am a partner in the firm of Teff & Co, solicitors representing Mrs Bloom and her family.'

He nodded at Tanzer Phillips and then said to Olive, 'We are both fully aware of your situation, Mrs Bell, and your two children. Can you let me see the birth certificates, which I understand you were asked to bring with you?'

Olive was pleased to see the two men. She would not be left alone with a hostile Mrs Bloom, and she considered there would be no scenes with this company.

She searched in her large handbag and brought out the two certificates. Mr Rose checked these before handing them to Mrs Bloom. She gave them a quick glance to check Ben had been named as the father and then placed them on one of the side tables.

Mr Rose invited Olive to give her story as to how she met

Ben, why she and Ben had kept their relationship secret from the family, whether they had intended to get married to legitimise the children and whether she was Jewish or would be content to convert for the sake of the children.

During this prelude, Mrs Bloom sat still, not voicing any comment. She gazed impassively ahead, not making any eye contact with Olive.

Olive, as brief as she could without leaving out the cardinal points, related her story of her meeting with Ben.

'At all times,' she said, 'it was Ben who had taken all the moves and had persuaded me to live with him. He knew I was Catholic and had been married and could not obtain a divorce from my church. But Ben had wanted to live and have a family with me. He had not felt able, due to his respect for his mother, to tell you'– she turned to Mrs Bloom – 'since he knew that you would not approve. He did not want to deceive you when he came to your Friday family evenings but he had not known how to approach the problem. It's wartime. He was in front line action and these are different times. Happiness was all that Ben wanted, and he felt I could give him this.

'I was in love with your son. We could not help ourselves. Now, regrettably, with Ben missing in action, I thought it right that Mrs Bloom should know she has two grandchildren.'

'Well, I suppose you thought of me because you want me to support you,' rasped Mrs Bloom without any form of pleasantness in her tone.

'Well, I thought you would want to meet with your grandchildren and, yes, I thought you would want to support them with Ben's money, which you receive as his next of kin. The reality is, Mrs Bloom, you have two grandchildren, the sons of Ben. Yes, I know that in Jewish law they aren't Jewish, but when they grow up they could convert and I'll be happy with any decision they'll come to in this regard. I fervently hope that the boys and I will be accepted in the family, as I have no family of my own.

'I pray for Ben's safety and hope that, when the war is over, Ben will be found in a POW camp and come home. This is what the adjutant at his air force station has said, and I pray that this will happen. Until then, I'm unable to work because I have to look after the children. I am, it is true, temporarily in financial difficulties. I will not be able to work until Paul will be at least eighteen months, when I could place him in a crèche. In the meantime, I really would appreciate anything you could do for your grandchildren.'

Olive stopped, having related all she could to Mrs Bloom about the history and situation in which she and Ben's children had found themselves. During this long explanation, Mrs Bloom had not spoken a word. Nor had she changed her expression from that of blank disinterest throughout the whole discourse. She had studiously avoided looking at Olive as she spoke, and she had not thrown a glance towards the infants.

There was a long pause lasting many seconds. To Olive, it seemed like minutes, although as she later realised it was probably some thirty seconds. This, in the circumstances, was a lengthy time. Presumably, she thought later, this was Mrs Bloom's thinking time as to her response.

Eventually, without looking at Olive, Mrs Bloom spoke – quietly at first but reaching an unacceptable volume in short time 'Olive ...' She looked down at the birth certificates. 'Mrs Bell, after years of living with my son in sin, as I would put it, after years without telling me or my family of your existence and now, when I'm mourning the loss or disappearance of my son, you come to me out of the blue with two children fathered by my son – who in any language are bastards – and claim them as my family. And then you want me to give you money to look after these bastards. I tell you, I won't do it.

'You didn't have the care to tell me of this terrible relationship. My son with a non-Jewish woman, a *shiksa,* and worse, a Catholic who is already married, and you come to me for money, for financial support. You made your bed with my son. Now you'll have to lie in it with all its consequences. You'll not hear from me. You'll not get a penny from me! I don't want to see you or your sons again. You bring me nothing but pain and aggravation. I want you to leave with these children now!' She gesticulated wildly with a dismissive sweep of her arm, as if she were removing the rubbish from her home.

At this, Adam Rose intervened, his words softer.

'Olive, you'll understand that Mrs Bloom is fraught at this moment. It appears more than possible that she has lost her elder son in the war. This in itself is heartbreaking. But now she finds that you and two grandchildren she had never before known of are here in her home. It is not surprising she is confused and angry at these events.

'Not unreasonably – and without any fault on your part – she is greatly disturbed that she had never been told of this relationship before. Being Jewish, she is naturally upset that her son lived with you, being Catholic and married without any real possibility of obtaining a divorce. Had you been free to do so, and if you were to have agreed to convert, then that would be the making of an acceptable family in a traditional Jewish home that Mrs Bloom is used to.

'We have, as you may have suspected, considered the alternatives. In all the circumstances, Mrs Bloom will accept that, if you will give up the children to her, she will obtain a nanny and they'll be brought up as part of her family and within the Jewish faith. If that will be the case, I shall deal with the legal formalities of adoption and payment by way of a generous lump sum to be made to you on completion of these formalities.

'This will enable you to start a new life with financial security. All we need, Mrs Bell, is your co-operation, and the matter can be dealt with in a few weeks. Naturally, Mrs Bloom will discharge all costs involved.'

Adam Rose concluded his comments with an encouraging nod and smile to Olive, willing her to accept.

Olive did not return his smile. She was dumbstruck, and she could not contain herself. She felt tears prickling her eyes. She paused and swallowed, and then her anger burst through. She looked directly at Mrs Bloom and, this time, Ben's mother met her eyes. She ignored Adam Rose and addressed herself to Mrs Bloom.

'I'd never thought in the wildest of my nightmares that I would visit Ben's mother in order to leave our children with her and never to see them again. And to be offered to be paid off is the final insult. You people have no idea of my thoughts and feelings. I'll never give up our children. I would never sell them off to obtain financial security!

'I didn't come here to obtain or ask for money for myself. I've come because I thought you would be interested in meeting and giving love to your grandchildren. They are in need of your support because I'm not Ben's next of kin and for the next year or so will be unable to work while looking after my and Ben's children.

'I find it deeply insulting you think I would give up my boys to you. I've no reason to stay any longer, and I've no intention of talking to you or meeting you again.'

At that, Olive picked up Kivi, wrapped his toys in the pram and went to the door.

Adam Rose tried to rescue the situation. 'Mrs Bell, don't be too hasty. We can resolve this matter.'

'I've heard quite enough, Mr Rose, to know that I don't belong in this house. I pray that Ben will return and we can have a great life together with our family. What he will want to do with his mother will be up to him but, from this day, I shall have nothing further to do with that woman.'

At that, Olive, with Kivi in hand, pushed the pram out of the room, down the hallway and saw herself out.

As she made her way home on the bus with the children, she pondered over her options, which were few. At this moment, she could not see her way ahead. At home, she made lunch for Kivi and prepared milk for Paul and a small salad for herself. She put the children in their cots for their afternoon sleep and fell on her bed. She could not restrain the tears that first fell and then streamed down her face. 'Oh Ben, what am I to do? Where am I going? Please come back to me!'

Two days later, she heard the bell ring in her flat. On opening the door, she was surprised to see Tanzer Phillips. He was alone, and Olive was curious as to why he would come. She waited while he stood on her doorstep and said, 'I've come alone, Olive. I want to have a word with you privately.' He paused. 'I have something constructive to say to you. It has absolutely nothing to do with that terrible morning at Mrs Bloom's house.'

'Do come in, Mr Phillips. I'm sorry I kept you on my doorstep, but I wasn't expecting to see you, especially after the last time. I'm sorry about the mess, but I can't run after Kivi all the time.'

Kivi was running around as she spoke, and Paul was lying quietly in his pram.

'Mr Phillips, I can't imagine why you're here after that terrible experience I had at Mrs Bloom's. But since you are here, can I get you a coffee or tea?

'You know, that would be very nice, perhaps a coffee. It has taken me more than an hour to find you, but I'm pleased to see you.'

He looked at Paul and refrained from disturbing him but played with Kivi on the floor with his toys. Olive brought over two cups of coffee with a small plate of biscuits.

'Now, let me say why I'm here, Olive. It certainly isn't to ask you to change your mind over what happened at Mrs Bloom's. I thought you were quite right to object to that proposal. It should never have been put to you. It was obscene by any standards.

'As you heard then, I was a very great friend of Kivi – Kivi senior, I had better say, looking at Kivi junior who has taken an interest at the mention of his name! We first worked together in the partnership, but I wanted to do other things and I left very amicably. We kept in touch closely over the years. I can't say I was close to Mrs Bloom, and you see how she can be.

'However, I remain as a warm friend of the family and simply loved the children. Ben was my favourite because he always knew what he wanted and worked hard to achieve it. I was an uncle he never had, although I know he had other "honorary" uncles.

'I have come here alone without anyone's knowledge, and I want you to keep this secret of mine.'

'Of course, Mr Phillips, I'm glad you've come. I'm still in shock over what happened at Mrs Bloom's.'

'Yes, I can imagine. I don't want you to take this the wrong way, and I want you to keep this just between ourselves. I know you are in financial difficulties and there is no one who can help you. You have, as they say, fallen through the gap in the legislation. I will go a long way to support Ben and certainly, in these tragic times we find ourselves in, his children. I am not without means, Olive. I'm an old man now, as you see, and I have no family left to support. I want you to accept a regular payment from me, and I want to start next week. Do you have a bank account?'

'Yes, I do, although I have to say I think there is just four pounds ten shillings in the account, left over from my last job.'

'Well, let me have your bank address and details of your account. I'm going to send to that account twenty pounds each month on the first of the month. That I hope will take care of your children and you until you can get yourself a job when little Paul has grown.'

'But this is so good of you, Mr Phillips.' Olive was overwhelmed. She had tears welling up in her eyes. Before she could utter another word, Tanzer, realising she was finding it difficult to maintain her composure, concluded, 'It's my pleasure and my debt to Ben. He would have wanted me to help in your circumstances.'

15

June–September 1945

At just after 10 a.m. on 11 June 1945, the telephone in Olive's flat rang. She was able to pick it up on the fifth ring.

'I would like to speak to Mrs Olive Bell, please.'

'Speaking, what can I do for you?'

'I'm Flight Lieutenant Whitmore, the adjutant at RAF Waterbeach. I've looked up our file on Sergeant Ben Bloom, and I understand my predecessor has been speaking to you on his case?'

'Yes, do you have news of Ben?' she enquired hastily.

'We received a telegram on the 26th of May from the Air Ministry. They had received a telegram from the International Red Cross Committee to the effect that Sergeant Bloom is believed to have lost his life on the night of 15–16 June 1944.

'On the second of June, we received a further letter from Air Ministry, stating that five crew members were buried in the parish cemetery at Rieux some five miles north-east of Cambrai, and a sixth was buried in the French civil cemetery at Iwuy close by. I'm sorry to tell you that there has been no body identified as Sergeant Bloom. After all this time, it has been concluded he must have perished in the crash.

'I'm sorry to be the bearer of bad news, but this information was forwarded on to Bloom's next of kin. However, there is a note on file from my predecessor that you should be contacted with any news of Sergeant Bloom.'

There was a pause. Olive was silent for a few seconds. *Is this the end of my quest to find Ben?* she asked herself. No, she instantly thought. While there was no body to be found, there remained hope. She would cling on to this hope. She reminded herself yet again that he could have lost his memory. He could still be in a camp. She would continue to search for him.

She answered in a calm voice. 'Thank you for your trouble in calling, Flight Lieutenant. I very much appreciate being kept informed. I still have no real evidence of Ben's death. It's all so circumstantial that I'll go on searching for information. If you were to hear anything, I should be grateful if you would continue to inform me. Thank you so much for calling'.

'I'm pleased to do so, but I wish I could give you better news, Mrs Bell.'

On 17 September, the adjutant forwarded a photograph to Olive which had been sent via the Air Ministry from a M Marliere of Cambrai. The photograph was of the communal grave at Rieux. Olive knew Ben was not buried there. But she knew that those who were had been Ben's colleagues. They had worked, eaten and drank together. Ben was missing from them. He *must* still be alive.

Ben, I will find you. I will never give up looking for you.

Olive wrote to M Marliere, explaining her interest in any information concerning the whereabouts of Ben or his body.

Marliere replied, telling her that Ben's aircraft had been shot down by a German night-fighter and that the crew must have been instantly killed when the plane crashed.

He said he had accompanied the local mayor when he had been summoned to witness the Germans taking the coffins from the crash site to the cemetery at Rieux. Local people had been kept out of the cemetery when the burial had taken place.

'However', he wrote, 'when the Germans had left, the local people covered the grave with flowers and a wreath was laid with many tri-colour ribbons and an inscription to the memory of brave Allied and British airmen. The Germans later removed the flowers. They were replaced again by the local people with a marble plaque with the inscription: To our bravest allies who gave up their lives for our liberation.

'This was also removed by the Germans.'

Marliere further reported that, 'Religious services had been held at both Rieux and Iwuy shortly after the burial, and these had been publicly announced from the pulpit by the parish priest, despite the danger in doing so. A great many people attended the services, even though a Gestapo unit and a German command post were based at nearby Cambrai. Allied bombing of Cambrai had resulted in the death and injury of many townsfolk, and a French-speaking German officer had remarked "French people are mad because they cover with flowers the graves of the airmen who killed them".'

December 1946

Kivi was nearly three and a half and was clutching Olive's hand as they walked together in the High Street of Enfield, shopping for warm winter clothes. She couldn't afford much, and the shops she went into were second hand – hand-me-downs for her and the children. She had a good eye, now well practised, and managed to scour the rails for clothes, however unfashionable, but which were at least presentable. Tanzer Phillips had died earlier that year, and with him died his payments to Olive.

Paul, now two, was in the buggy and was sleeping. They had been in Enfield for less than an hour when she was accosted by a woman whom at first she did not recognise –

mainly she thought later because she had never expected to see her.

'It is Olive, isn't it? You must be Olive. Don't you recognise me?' And after a short pause, she said, 'I'm Mary Bell, Arthur's mother. Now you remember.'

Olive looked carefully at Mary and, although she had changed over the few years since they had last met, she recognised her husband's mother.

'Of course I do. How are you? You look good.'

'Yes, life's treated me well. Arthur will be pleased I met you. Look, let me buy you a coffee and perhaps the children would like a bun or two. I should like to catch up with your news.'

And so they walked together to a nearby cafe called The Cabin, where wives and young students met for coffee and soft drinks. They sat down around the table for a talk about the past. Olive had always got on with Mary, so there was no bad history between them. She knew that Mary was aware her son had deserted her to live with another woman, and that he had never contacted Olive since leaving her. Mrs Bell also knew the marriage had not been kind to Olive.

Over hot coffee, and with Kivi eating a cream bun with chocolate which he had chosen and Paul chewing on a chocolate biscuit, they told each other of their recent past. Olive reminisced about Ben. She had received no further information as to his whereabouts, and he was presumed dead by the RAF. They had advised her that his name was to be included in the memorial being proposed to be built at Runnymede for all those missing and presumed dead – and whose bodies had never been found.

Pointing to Kivi and Paul, Olive told Mary they were Ben's children and she had not been able to marry him as she could not obtain a divorce through the church. 'This is Kivi, now three, aren't you, Kivi?'

Kivi looked at Mary Bell with his dark blue eyes. 'I'm three and a half,' he corrected.

'And so you are, you look such a big boy, Kivi,' Mary said encouragingly. 'And who is your brother?'

'He's Paul. He's two and a bit. He's usually sleeping,' Kivi explained.

'You're lucky, Olive. I should love to have a grandchild, but Arthur's still single and without children. He's often spoken of you. He has matured, Olive. He's a different person to the one you knew. War changed him. I know how he mistreated you and there's no excuse for what he did. But he's a different person now. He never stayed with Helen, you know. He was stupid. He was drinking too much at that time. He'd love to meet you. He often speaks well of you and how much he misses you. Can I suggest to him that he calls you? You might find him more than agreeable. There was something between you in the early part of your marriage. It'll be there now. He could at least look after you and the children if you were to go back together. Let me ask him to call you.'

Olive gave Mary her telephone number and address.

'See how it goes. You never know. It could be a renewal of your marriage! It doesn't seem likely that Ben survived the war. Even the RAF has given up.'

Four days later, Olive received a call from Arthur. Arthur was comforting on the phone and was eager to meet her.

'Look, much water has passed under the bridge since we broke up. Let's see what can be managed between us. I'm really keen to see you. I'm sure we can make a go of it. I should be glad to take on the boys, and maybe we can have one ourselves. We're still married so we've nothing to lose.'

Olive's defences were non-existent. She recalled with horror the beatings she had suffered from him and how he had walked out having left her a note on the kitchen table all those years ago. She also recalled she had felt relieved. But had he changed? He had said so. Mary had said so. He, at least, had recognised his problems and seemed happy to have put them to bed. More important, he had said he would want to look after the boys.

Having been rejected by the Bloom family, Olive was in great need of support – financial as well as moral. In Arthur, if indeed he had changed, she may have found her answer. If Arthur could be the man she first met when she was happy with him in those early days then all might come good after all. She had nothing else to look forward to, and this could prove to be the secure support she needed.

'Arthur, why don't we meet? Come over here and we can go out with the children and see how things are together.'

'Fine, Olive. That would be perfect. How about Saturday? I could be with you at eleven. We can go into the country, walk with the children and enjoy lunch together. Is that okay?'

'Sounds great, Arthur. I look forward to seeing you.'

Saturday came and Olive, to her surprise, found herself quite excited and looking forward to seeing Arthur. After the call and his mother's assurance, she was not nervous, remembering the early days of her marriage.

Before he arrived, Olive looked into the mirror. She put on some make-up and selected a pretty necklace. When the doorbell rang, she felt as if she were seventeen again. He looked older than she expected. But then it had been over nine years. She knew she had aged too and hoped this would not put him off. It didn't seem to as he entered her small flat. His old charm was apparent.

'Olive, you haven't changed. You look as I remember you – slim, beautiful and always smiling.' He gave her a kiss on her cheek and then, having squeezed her gently around her shoulders, kissed her again lightly on the lips.

Olive acknowledged this by returning a kiss on the tip of his nose and laughing. She thought they were acting like teenagers going out for the first time.

Hopefully he had lost his angst, she thought, and certainly there was no hint of it when he came into the sitting room where the two boys were playing with their toys. Olive introduced them, and Arthur immediately took an interest in them, playing with them and holding them upside down to their screams of enjoyment.

'Now don't spoil them, Arthur. They'll expect you to play with them every time they see you.'

'That'll be fine with me,' he quickly answered, looking at Olive with affection in his eyes.

The boys climbed into the back of Arthur's Ford 8 and Olive gave them some toys to play with which would keep them occupied during the journey. They left South Woodford and drove into the countryside. They stopped in the village of Hexton, where laburnum trees lined its main street. For lunch, they found a quaint old oak-beamed hostelry with old-style wooden tables.

It sold bottled beer, which Arthur ordered for himself, and a glass of house white wine for Olive. The boys each had a glass of orangeade, a great treat for them.

Over lunch, Arthur pressed his case. 'It's been a long time, Olive. Too long. I know it was my fault you left. I never blamed you. But we were both caught in the same problem of Catholic abhorrence to divorce. Now we have a second chance, and I hope you'll find it in your heart to accept the challenge. I really think we had something going for us. I believe we can make a successful go of it.

'I know about Ben and I'm sorry that you had to go through the torment of his disappearance and death in the war. Now here we are together, Olive, in a different world. I'll be pleased to bring up your children as if they're mine and well, Olive, you never know,' he said with a smile and twinkle in his eyes. 'We just may have our own to join them.'

'Let me think on it. It's a major decision for both of us, and I need to know that you won't go back to how you were before. I need to be comforted this time around, and not only comfort but some security. I cannot be left like last time. Maybe you can consider adopting the children? And I'll need some sort of agreement which will grant me maintenance during our living together and later if we were to part. I need this security because I'll have to give up my income I've been receiving from the charity. I'll have to give up my flat. You see where I'm coming from? I have to protect my family, and this will be your family as well.'

'Sure, Olive. I'm not without means. I'll look after you. We can sort this out with a solicitor and put your mind at rest. If this is settled, can I take it that we can get back together as a family? Let's give ourselves a few weeks to renew our relationship. I'm very keen to start over again. I know we can make a go of it.'

Perhaps it was because it was the end of the war, when decisions were taken quickly, that she accepted Arthur's offer so easily. Most people had not been able to make joint decisions during the war. Husbands were away doing the fighting and communication was difficult. By the time one could discuss anything, the moment had passed and the question seemed irrelevant in the circumstances of the war. Decisions had been made for everyone because there were only utility goods and clothes in the shops. Rationing, even after the war, was very strictly controlled and choices limited, so one existed and lived the best way one could.

Decisions were made as to the next film to see at the Troxy Cinema or the dance at the local Savoy rooms with the band of Stanley Goode. Olive, not finding it easy to obtaining babysitters, had found it more than difficult to go out to these high points of living. She amused herself with radio programmes like *Itma* and *Round the Horne*. Even *Dick Barton Special Agent* became a favourite at 6.45 each evening.

After just a few weeks and several evenings and weekends with Arthur, Olive was convinced she could take that decision. She certainly – and desperately – needed male company – someone at home, someone she could talk to and share mutual problems with and who would be kind to her and the children. She did not think lightning struck twice and this time, having learned lessons from the past, Arthur would surely be the changed person he had been keen to show Olive he had become.

The boys needed a father figure and, all in all, Arthur seemed to be her man. He had matured. He had changed for the better, and she thought she could rely on his new-found confidence in life.

She had loved Arthur when they first met. She had adored him when they married, and the first months had all been a feast of love and excited anticipation. Olive later considered that the subsequent failure in the marriage was due to the stress of losing his job and his concerns for his dignity and ability to look after themselves in a manner which they had come to accept. His anger had come, she thought, from his frustrations and sense of failure. And this had triggered his violence towards her.

But a new world was dawning now in 1946, and Arthur looked like another man with the confidence that an acceptable well-paid job in the building industry gave to him. His kind and soft manner underlined this new confidence.

He happily settled the agreed maintenance for her and the boys, should anything happen to him or in the case of a separation. This time, Olive would not be sent on to the streets penniless. This was now inscribed in legal documents, binding and enforceable. She fervently hoped that this pre-condition she had required before moving in with Arthur would never come about. There seemed no reason why it should. They found the love between them that they had enjoyed all those years ago when they had first settled.

So 1946 moved into 1947, and life for Olive was bliss. Arthur was kind towards her and with Kivi and Paul. She became pregnant, and they both had the joy of parenthood when Gregory was born in the summer.

But Arthur soon became preoccupied with Gregory. He doted on the baby and began to exclude Olive and her sons from his attention and love. As Olive began to reproach him for this attitude, which was dividing the family, he grew morose and vindictive in his responses.

It was Saturday, 1 November 1947, when Arthur first exploded with rage. He'd had a very bad week with his business. Government controls, which he had evaded in order to complete a contract, had caught up with him. There was an ongoing investigation, and he could lose his position and be barred from future contracts. He couldn't take stress and when, during the morning, Kivi and Paul had been shouting and fighting Arthur lost patience and bundled them into the small dark cupboard under the stairs and locked the door. The children were frightened. Having to listen to their screams, Olive remonstrated with him.

'Olive, keep out of this. The boys need training and discipline, and I'm about to deliver it. They have to learn to be quiet when told.'

'But they're only young boys, Arthur. No need to treat them so severely.'

'What do you know about discipline and order? You keep out of it. This is *my* province.'

'Arthur, you're not to touch my boys. I'll discipline them, not you. They weren't doing anything bad.'

'Don't argue with me. They're not your boys in this house. I'm responsible for them, and they'll have to learn how to behave in my house!' He was shouting and almost out of control.

'Arthur, calm down and let the boys out. They're frightened. They're really crying. I'll talk to them. They're my boys.'

Arthur had completely lost his temper now. He screamed at Olive, 'They're as much my boys as yours now. I'm paying for their keep. I'll discipline them as I think best. They need a bloody good hiding, and I'll give them one when I get them out of that cupboard, but they can stay there for the next hour and give me some peace.'

Olive went to the cupboard to turn the key and open the door. Arthur struck her hard on her back, which sent her flying to the floor. She lay on the floor, stunned. Arthur, now totally out of control, lifted her up by the collar of her dress and swung his arm, hitting her with his open palm across her face and knocking her down again. Blood appeared from Olive's lip and she screamed in pain. Arthur gave her stricken body on the floor a strong kick in the side, which made her cry out uncontrollably. He left her lying on the floor.

'Don't fuck with me. You'll leave the boys where they are until I allow them to come out.'

Olive managed to crawl to bed and try to recover. She knew Arthur was under pressure. Perhaps he was not wholly to blame for his actions. She thought of every excuse for his conduct, and she did not want to break up with him. If she could, she would stay and try to calm his anger. He would know what the consequences of his business actions would be in the next few weeks. If they turned out satisfactory for him, Olive thought he would recover from his anxieties, which she believed was the cause of his violence towards her and the boys.

Olive knew that Arthur, under the pressure at work, could not cope with everyday life. He was continually short-tempered. The boys were terrified of him, and Olive helped them to keep away and out of his presence as much as possible. He only had time for Gregory.

Over the next two weeks, Olive was the victim of a number of beatings, which Arthur gave when he took quick offence. She had no one to turn to and thought there might be no end to his behaviour. She was more concerned with his attitude towards Kivi and Paul, whom he had begun to beat harshly too. *How would this end?* Olive had hoped Arthur would come to realise his actions were wholly unacceptable, and that he could return to the kindness he had shown in the early days of their reunion.

But Olive had to make immediate decisions. If she took her three boys, she knew that Arthur would go to extremes to get Gregory, his own child, back. He would, she knew, be out of his mind with rage. He would be uncontrollable. In such a rage, Olive could envisage him going so far as to mutilate or even kill her, or do serious damage to Ben's boys. She knew she had to make a decision. She had no time to consider all the arguments.

She realised Arthur had brought about the reunion in order to have her bear him a child. He was only interested in Gregory. Olive felt in the coldness of her logic that she could only obtain a form of peace if she left with Kivi and Paul. How could she leave her baby? It was no judgement of Solomon, as clarity told her that she would have to forfeit Gregory to ensure the safety and future of Kivi and Paul and indeed herself.

Before making an irrevocable decision, she decided to talk with Mary. It had been Mary who had reconciled them. It had been she who had persuaded Olive to give Arthur another chance, after all. Perhaps this would be the last chance she had of saving her marriage a second time. However, when she spoke with Mary and showed her discolouring bruises, she did not meet with a great deal of sympathy or support.

'You know, you always were a bit of a nag, Olive. My son can't stand that, and it brings on his problems. He has lots to worry about and doesn't need domestic upsets at the same time. You should be more loving towards him.'

Olive felt there was nothing further she could say.

Kivi had come, weeping, to her for a cuddle, and between his sobs said, 'Mummy, I don't like Daddy. He's so nasty to Paul and me. He hits us all the time. I don't want to live here. Can't we go back to where we used to live?'

Olive kissed him tenderly and said, 'Everything will be

all right. I'll look after you and Paul. If he hits you again, I'll take you both away from him.'

'Thanks, Mummy. I don't want to upset you, but we don't want to live here with him.'

Olive promised herself that if he beat her or the boys again, she would leave. It happened that very evening; she went to bed nursing her arms and legs, where he had brutally hit and kicked her as she lay on the floor.

The following morning, Olive went looking for a flat for herself and Ben's boys. She well knew that, if she were to take Gregory, Arthur would come after her, and she could not take this risk. When she returned home, she found her key would not turn in the lock. She tried several times before she realised the lock must have been changed by Arthur. She was locked out of her house, with her boys inside. She began to knock frantically at the door, and screamed and shouted for her children. Janet McCarthy, her neighbour from four houses down, came out to see what the noise was all about.

'I've been locked out by Arthur. He's changed the locks. My boys are inside.' Olive was in tears, uncontrollably weeping.

Janet McCarthy well knew the problems between Olive and Arthur. Indeed, all the street had been made aware. Janet told Olive she was calling the police. 'The boys may be in danger in his present mood.'

Two constables arrived. They managed to get Mary, who was in the house, to open up. Olive clutched hold of Kivi and Paul, but Mary told the constables that her son had changed the locks and was in fear that Olive was about to take the three children with her. In tears, Olive cried she had no thought of taking Gregory but had to leave with her two boys as Arthur was beating them – and her. Janet told the policemen that it was common knowledge in the street that Arthur had regularly hit both Olive and the children, as they had heard the screams from time to time.

Janet, looking purposefully at Mary, said, 'Olive, we all know what's going on. You'll be safer if you stayed with me and my husband tonight so you can make arrangements tomorrow.'

The lead policeman spoke to Olive. 'It appears, madam, that this is a matrimonial dispute and we can't interfere.' But he warned Mary that Olive had every right to have the return of her children and that she, Mary, had to arrange this by the next morning.

Olive stayed with Janet and her husband, Mike, that night. She did not sleep. She tossed and turned, and her mind was in turmoil. Arthur was clearly unable to rid himself of his demons. Olive realised that he could not take pressure – of any description – and, if he had a bad day at the office, he would take it out on her and Ben's boys. He wouldn't touch Gregory.

She knew she couldn't live like this. It had happened before, not just once but on too many occasions and, as she lay in the warmth of the bed that Janet and Mike had provided for her, she realised she could not spend the rest of her life with Arthur. The marriage had to end. She had to get Ben's boys back and, although she loved Gregory fiercely, she knew Arthur and his mother would fight tooth and nail for him. She had already told Janet she could never win that argument. She felt Arthur had married her in order to have a child of his own, and she wouldn't deprive him of that gift.

Olive's mind returned to Ben. She thought of all the wonderful times they had enjoyed together, and the love that he had centred on her, particularly when Kivi had been born.

He had been so happy when she fell pregnant with their second child, and she remembered the warm moments when they had fun discussing the names they would choose for the second child. They had both thought the second child would be a daughter, and the biblical name of Talia was considered the most acceptable. When Paul arrived, he was a surprise, but by then Ben was missing in action.

In her bed that night, Olive kept thinking of Ben. Just suppose he was still alive. Anything was possible. The RAF had tried to assure her that, after all this time, he could not have survived. They had approached all hospitals and nursing homes in France, particularly in Normandy and the Pas de Calais areas, to see whether any British serviceman had been taken in with wounds, but there had been no positive response. Following liberation, French local authorities had been asked whether they had anyone in their midst who could have come from the Allied forces in whatever physical or mental condition. There had been a few, but all those had been identified and brought back to their families. There had been no news of Ben. For the thousandth time, Olive asked herself how Ben could have vanished off the face of the world when the bodies of his six crew members had been identified and had received a proper burial?

She had no answer, and seemingly no one else had either. But there and then, between the sheets of the bed, she made a solemn personal oath that she would spend as much time as possible in finding him. He was not to lie unknown and cold in the earth somewhere in Normandy, like a lost soldier of the '14–18 war, where so many had died in the mud of Flanders.

As dawn began to break and the room lightened, Olive cleared her mind. *First I must find a job. Then I must obtain a home. And only then can I take back Ben's boys.* She decided she would see a solicitor at the first opportunity to look at the agreement Arthur had signed for maintenance for her and the children in the event of the marriage breaking up. It was not an act of revenge. She felt none. She realised Arthur was not his own master when pressures took hold of him. But she wanted some form of security for her and the two boys, and felt she deserved this.

She dressed quickly and had a breakfast of coffee and a slice of bread buttered with marmalade. She told Janet, 'After I've settled Kivi and Paul at the welfare home, I'm going straight to the council offices to register for a flat with two bedrooms. Until I get it, I can't look after the boys. And then I'm going to a solicitor to sort myself out with Arthur.'

'Good, Olive! There's no future for you with that man. If you need me to support you with evidence, you can rely on me.'

'Thanks, Janet. I really appreciate your support. However, the first thing is for me to get hold of Kivi and Paul. The police told me last night I should take them to the welfare home. They even gave me the address. Could you come with me? I'm nervous of seeing Mary alone. I presume Arthur will be at his office.'

'Sure, Olive. Let's go as soon as possible'.

Mary did not put up a fight. Having heard what the police had said the previous evening, she had told Arthur that he had to give up the two boys, but she said she would hang on to Gregory whatever happened.

So, reasonably peacefully, Mary gave up Kivi and Paul to Olive. She looked sullen, but obviously did not want to have an argument in front of Janet.

Olive took them to the children's home in the clothes they were wearing. It took more than two hours for her to register the boys, having presented their birth certificates to confirm they were her sons. Accompanied by a young and helpful care assistant, she had taken them to their room and showed them around the children's home. Olive had explained the reasons for their having to live at the home, just until she could get a flat from the council. Kivi and Paul were only too pleased to be out of the clutches of Arthur, and so were not at all put out at having to live at the home without their mother for a while.

At the town hall, Olive met with negative response.

'Mrs Bell, I'm sorry I can't be more helpful. There's a major strain on our housing resources now that the war's over. There's so much bomb damage around the country and such a shortage of housing. You're currently on a priority list. You really must get your husband to take you back.'

'You don't understand. I've left my husband because he threw me out, and more importantly because I could no longer cope with beatings. I have two children from another relationship – their father is missing and presumed dead by the RAF – and they are parked in a welfare home away from me. I need to give them a home.'

'Maybe, maybe, Mrs Bell. But we're not magicians. We can't build more homes right here in this office. I'll make sure you get on the list, but you'll have to wait your turn. Your advantage is that you have two young children who'll be better off with you than in the home. If anything turns up, you'll hear from us.'

The next step for Olive was to go to the Labour Exchange. 'Any job will do,' she said desperately. 'I'm best at admin. I was a solicitor's clerk looking after their administration and accounts during the war until my babies arrived. Have you anything on your books?'

Olive's heart sank as she watched the official take a few notes down on his large notepad. She knew he was just going through the motions. The next person in the queue coughed impatiently.

'I wish I had, Mrs Bell. There are thousands of men and women coming out of the services who all want jobs. There aren't many jobs around, and those who had jobs before their call-up have priority to get their old jobs back. I'll put you on the lists and suggest you call in from time to time to check if anything suitable comes in.'

'I'm not choosy. I'll accept anything within reason. I need to work. I *need* to earn to keep my children.'

'I'm sure something will come up for you. Just keep looking,' the official, in a white shirt and drab tie, said unconvincingly and, without another look at Olive, turned to a new file and called the next person in line.

Olive's next step was to find a solicitor's office. She knew where they were for the most part. She was always surprised that so many firms could be found in the same street. Rather like antique shops, she thought. She supposed that they congregated together so the public could take their pick. And this was exactly what Olive did.

She declined to go into the smallest and shabbiest of offices, and she also avoided the more magnificent early eighteenth-century buildings with pretentious steps leading into Georgian buildings. This would surely be for wealthy country farmers and developers and not for the likes of her.

She chose a modest firm in a dignified two-storey building with three names of the partners on the brass nameplate adjacent to the front door.

She went to reception where a young girl of no more than seventeen years, and suitably dressed in a shirt, smart black jumper and shortish skirt, greeted her.

'I need to see a solicitor about a maintenance agreement. I have it with me,' Olive said, taking the document out of her handbag as if to show her credentials. 'My name is Mrs Bell, Olive Bell,' she added.

'Have you been here before? If so, who have you seen?'

'No, this is my first visit.'

'Well, then I suggest you may wish to see Mr Parkin. He's the junior partner who looks after matrimonial matters.'

Olive nodded and the confident young girl called Mr Parkin on the intercom.

'I have a client here who needs advice on a maintenance agreement. She has it with her.' There was a pause. 'Yes, her name is Mrs Bell, Olive Bell.' Another pause and then 'Yes, sir'.

The young receptionist turned to Olive. 'If you don't mind waiting a little, Mr Parkin will see you shortly. It might be fifteen minutes. Will that be all right?'

'Yes, that's fine.' Olive moved to the rear of the room, sat in a comfortable chair and picked up the *Express*.

It was a little over fifteen minutes, just as she was getting absorbed in a news story about a grisly murder, when the receptionist told her to go upstairs to the door with Mr Parkin's name on.

She found Hubert Parkin, some thirty-five years old with receding hair at the temples leading into a bald patch, sitting behind an imposing desk which seemed too large for a junior partner. He was dressed as she expected, in a dark, well-tailored suit and pleasing tie to match, a starched white shirt and collar. He was sitting in a tall-backed chair with deep red upholstery. He spoke in a higher pitched voice than she would have expected. But his vowels were clear cut, almost with affectation, and with no regional accent. He purred class and learning. He might well be the man she required, Olive thought. He was warm in his opening comments and appeared to be keen to listen.

'Good morning, Mrs Bell, and what can I do for you?' he enquired politely.

Olive presented the maintenance agreement to him and, while he was reading it, she gave a short history of her marriage, separation and return to Arthur Bell – and the acts which required her to leave again.

'There shouldn't be too great a difficulty in enforcing this agreement. I shall have to take a statement from you, which you can sign. It will be helpful if you have witnesses who can verify your statement as to the cause of the latest breakdown of the marriage. The problem may arise if Mr Bell has no means. We cannot enforce an agreement when the respondent has no means with which to make payments.'

'Well, Mr Parkin, he has a good job as director of a building company, which pays well. He has kept the child we had together, my youngest, Gregory, but I have taken the two boys I had with the late Ben Bloom whom you see, Mr Parkin, he agreed to support.'

'Well then, let's see what we can do.' At this, he brought in his secretary and dictated a firm and forceful letter addressed to Arthur Bell, threatening service of a summons if payments had not commenced in accordance with the agreement within seven days.

'Come and see me in ten days and let me know if your account has been credited with this sum. If you care to stay in reception for a few minutes, my secretary will give you a copy of this letter. You must let me know when you receive this first payment – and I'm sorry, but there will be a charge for our services. We cannot get it from your husband at this stage, but if this matter were to go to court, then we can ask for costs, which I think we should be able to get for you.'

Mr Parkin stood and came around his desk to show Olive out.

Within four days, Olive checked and discovered that the first payment had been made. She immediately called to see Mr Parkin and settled his firm's account. Now she could look for a decent flat and could arrange to take on a job – one with enough income to look after her and her boys.

16

May 1948

After what had seemed like months of searching, Olive had eventually found a job at the council's offices working in the planning department. It was secure. The pay was adequate and, with the maintenance Arthur was paying, she could manage. She still did not have a flat, and the two boys remained in the children's home run by the council. She had pressed as much as she thought she could to raise her position on the housing list, but still she remained waiting, without great hope of an early deliverance. She had found a room for herself at a boarding house and was acceptably comfortable there. She visited the boys every early evening and had time to read to them. Kivi was taken to the primary school each morning, while Paul attended a kindergarten within the children's home.

At weekends, Olive was able to take them out, but living like this was distressing her. She was in a low state but kept her mind on her job since she knew very well she could not afford to have a breakdown and lose the position. However, daily strain began to tell. She was alone, no family, no one to comfort her and, worse still, she could not see her future with any clarity. She lost her appetite and, accordingly, lost weight. It was late in May, weakened after weeks of not eating a proper meal, that she passed out while at work.

Her colleagues tried to revive her and laid her on a couch and called a doctor. She was taken immediately to the local hospital, where her rundown body was treated. It was the hospital report that enabled the housing director to grant her a two-bedroom council flat.

Following her treatment and recovery, she was able at last to bring both Kivi and Paul to live with her. They were so happy to be reunited with their mother and to be able to live in a flat and not an institution. Olive's spirits were raised and she began, after so many months of despair, to reorganise her life.

Three weeks later, she looked much better so her doctor allowed her to return to her work in the council offices. The flat was newly built in a block of eight. There were six other blocks in the immediate vicinity in a surround of green parkland. It was perfect for the boys to play football. There were other families in her block, so company for Olive and the children was on tap. The flat had been completed only two years before, and Olive and the boys were only the second family to have lived there. At last, she could feel the comfort of security.

She presented the boys with toys and new clothes and spoiled them grandly in the first weeks in their new home. She had no problems in making arrangements for them to return to a neighbour's flat for the hour or so in the afternoon before she could leave her work. *At last,* Olive thought, *I have a home and am with my children.*

During the summer of 1948, her attention returned to Ben and his possible whereabouts. She spoke with the adjutant of RAF Waterbeach and asked for further assistance in her search for Ben. He replied that, regrettably, he was not in a position to help her himself. He recommended that she write to personnel management at RAF Innsworth Gloucester and to set out her position.

This she did, and it took just under a fortnight to receive a reply. It was a full and helpful letter, so far as it could go. The officer dealing with Olive's letter was sympathetic. He pointed out that letters from Wing Commander Wyatt and also the station padre had been sent to the next of kin in accordance with the regulations. These had been issued immediately following the formal acknowledgement of Ben's missing in action in June 1944.

The letter also stated that Ben Bloom was to be commemorated at the RAF war memorial at Runnymede on Panel 235, which confirmed that his body had not been located.

In early September 1948, Olive received a letter from the Air Ministry after further attempts to obtain information. There, in a letter dated 31 August, she learned for the first time that there were two Lancasters that had crashed in the same area on that early morning. The letter explained that, following a special RAF Missing Research and Enquiry Office discussion in France, exhumation had been undertaken. The remainder of Ben's crew and those seven of the second crew had been accounted for, but there was still no evidence of Ben's burial in Rieux or elsewhere.

Over the years, Olive had never forgotten her quest to find the last resting place of Ben. She continued to write letters to the Air Ministry and to various air force departments who had interest in the death and remembrances of wartime airmen who had been killed or went missing during the war. These were the departments with whom she had built up a file of correspondence following Rabbi Weitzman's recommendations, now many years previously.

But all to no avail. In the meantime, blessed with a good job and rising in the hierarchy of the local government in the planning department, Olive had managed her life in a secure manner, which she found satisfying and gave her the stability she not had since her days with Ben.

17

May 1995

Olive had earned the respect and admiration of the parents of her children's friends for bringing up the boys alone. It was through these social connections from the school parents' meetings that she met Frank and Kitty Humphrey. They became particular friends and entertained both her and the boys on a regular basis. It helped, of course, that Kivi was a close friend of their son, James.

It was a May morning in 1995, light and warm without being hot, when Frank spoke to Olive.

'You know, I should like to help you in your efforts to find out what happened to Ben. I don't know in which direction, but I'm fairly free these days and I can travel and do some research where needed. I could always act as your driver. Kitty and I think you're really marvellous to continue looking for Ben. Most would have given up by now. We look upon it as a long-standing romantic love affair. Anything that we can do to help you, we shall, Olive.'

'I really appreciate it, Frank. I'm sure there'll come a time when I'll need your advice and support. I'll certainly keep you involved.'

Indeed, she wrote, with Frank's advice, to everyone who might conceivably help her, including her member of parliament. Nothing of any real value came back to her although she realised that the various departments had given of their time and had eventually, as she accepted, assiduously given her all information at their disposal. Some had made suggestions as to whom she might consider approaching further, which she did. But after all her endeavours, she was still none the wiser.

Frank and Olive paid visits to the RAF Museum at Hendon to check further and obtain advice from the research and information services. They also visited the Air Historical Branch at RAF Northolt, and further time was given to a visit to the records at Kew to check the operations record book of No. 514 Squadron and the Group ORB. Nothing further by way of useful information was obtained, however.

Frank suggested they check with Ben's family as to whether they obtained further information about his death and remains since, as next of kin, they would be given any such information. Olive had had no contact with them since that terrible day when she removed herself from the home of Ben's mother. She did not feel she could reopen that painful wound and Pam, Paul's wife, said she would do the research to find those surviving.

Pam found that, after 1945, Ben's mother and family had moved from the address Olive had visited. She managed to find another address from the War Graves Commission, but Pam's further enquiries revealed that they had left that address in 1951. All further enquiries proved fruitless, and she had to tell Olive and Frank that that particular avenue was closed. Ben's mother, she thought, would certainly not have survived to the 1990s, and so Pam thought the only way ahead was to write to the Mayor of Rieux, setting out Olive's quest for information about Ben's whereabouts, as he had clearly died in the Lancaster that had crashed in the early hours of 16 June 1944. This Olive did, setting out all the relevant information she possessed and details as to Ben's sons and her position – and her failed attempts to find this information for over fifty years. She wrote that it may well be her last chance of ascertaining what really happened to Ben.

The mayor replied that he and his colleagues would be very pleased to see Olive and her friends on such a quest. He said he would ensure they could meet with the archivist and local historians of both Rieux and neighbouring Iwuy. He would brief them as to Olive's problem.

On 23 May 1995, Olive, accompanied by Frank and Kitty Humphrey and Pam, arrived in Rieux, a typical small French town, charming in its layout with the *mairie* centrepiece. They immediately went to the *mairie* and Pam explained to the receptionist that they had arrived to meet with the mayor.

'*D'accord. Le Maire vous accueillera.*' Reverting into broken English, she guided them into the Salon du Maire. 'This way, please'.

The mayor, resplendent in his tailcoat and republican sash across his rather portly frame, came around his large and imposing desk to greet Olive and the others. He kissed Olive in the French manner on both cheeks and introduced her to Ernest Capliez and Cyriaque Colpart from the Historical Society in Rieux and its greater area, which included the nearby larger town of Iwuy. He then shook hands with Pam, Frank and Kitty and offered them chairs in line behind Olive.

Speaking in a strong French accent, the mayor commenced proceedings with an apology. 'I am sorry for my bad English but' – he paused to look at Olive and smiled – 'it may be preferable than to speak in my native tongue.' He assured Olive that both Ernest and Cyriaque spoke better English than he, at which he gave a hearty laugh. The other two Frenchmen joined in, and the English four smiled in acknowledgement.

'You, Madame,' he said, looking at Olive, 'have pursued with great courage and single mindedness your ambition to find the body of your late husband.'

Neither Olive nor the others wished to correct him. He was in full flow of language. 'And your efforts hopefully will not be in vain! To us, in Rieux, we salute you on your brave husband's behalf and those of his comrades who lost their lives in the fight for freedom and the liberation of our country from Nazi occupation. It is with admiration that we greet an Englishwoman who searches for the body of her husband, even fifty years since the war. It is a love story supreme. We salute you!' At which the mayor gave Olive a portly bow. Olive smiled gently at him in acknowledgement.

He continued, 'Monsieur Capliez is the archivist for this area and well knows the history of that night, and Monsieur Colpart is a historian for the Cambrai area and wishes to write an article of the terrible happenings of the night of the 15th and 16th of June 1944. This will be published in *Cambrai Historical Magazine* and will receive great publicity in this larger area. It may well prompt memories of the people who may have witnessed or heard talk of what actually occurred. I now wish you to listen to Monsieur Capliez, who has studied the actions of that night.'

M Capliez, a tall, lean and balding man wearing glasses with thick lenses on a gaunt-looking but friendly face, rose from his chair and gave a short bow both to the mayor, who had resumed his chair behind the grand desk, and also to Olive.

He began speaking fluent English without an accent.

'It has been some years since I first looked into this particular case. It is surprising to us that, while five of the crew of that stricken plane were buried in the cemetery of

Rieux, and one body was found in the fields of our neighbouring town, Iwuy, the seventh body, being your husband, was apparently never found. At least never buried with his comrades.

'I have been advised by those who witnessed the action that night that a number of Lancaster bombers, which had earlier bombed the railyards at Valenciennes, were returning to England and were above us. At about 0015, the German guns go into action. We do not know what exactly happened, but two planes were either shot down or collided attempting to avoid the gunfire – or even perhaps downed by German night-fighters. The plane, later identified as the one your husband was in, skimmed the roofs of the houses of Iwuy and crashed some one hundred and fifty metres from the north-east boundary, forming a large crater.

'The point of impact is still visible today and is on the property now owned by Monsieur Pierre Dagniaux of rue La Fayette. There were no survivors. Madame Olive, we can be assured that the pilot, knowing he was flying over a built-up area, did all in his power to avoid crashing on the town. The whole crew deserve the gratitude of the population.

'Five of the crew were buried with the consent of the Germans in the Rieux cemetery. A sixth body was found by school children later the next day in a cornfield, a few kilometres away and closer to the town of Iwuy. He was buried the following day in the civil cemetery at Iwuy. That body was acknowledged by his name tag as being Sergeant Hutt. But there was no mention of the seventh member of the crew, being your husband, Sergeant Bloom. You may wish to visit the site at which his plane crashed and which clearly must have been the place of his death. I have spoken to Monsieur Dagniaux, who would be honoured if you choose to visit this site where the indenture in the ground made by the impact of the Lancaster can still be clearly seen.'

Before they took leave of the mayor, Cyriaque Colpart stood and, with a small bow to Olive, said it was a great honour to have met the widow of Sergeant Benjamin Bloom.

'It has been agreed,' he said, 'with the *Cambrai Historical Magazine* that I write a chapter in memory of Sergeant Benjamin Bloom. This magazine has a wide circulation and those in the Iwuy area will certainly read it as it is of great interest to them. It may well prompt memories, and there will be a comment at the end inviting readers to relate any recollections they may have to me.

'If anything constructive comes to light, I shall advise the mayor and you will be most certainly informed. Please do not give up in your long quest to find the body of your late husband.

'If you agree, I should like to travel with my colleague and lead you to the exact place where your late husband's plane crashed and where he lost his life in his fight for freedom. Perhaps,' he said, looking at Frank Humphrey, 'you will be kind enough to follow us in our car?' He bowed both towards Olive and the mayor.

The mayor stood and everyone else followed. But before anyone could put a foot forward for the departure, the mayor, smiling at his guests from England, said, 'I cannot let you leave without a toast to you all for taking the time to visit us in Rieux. You must all have *une verre du vin* in honour of your visit.'

Looking directly at Olive, he bowed again, saying in his French-accented English, 'Madame Olive, you do us honour in Rieux to have taken some fifty years in trying to trace your late husband. He fought with great honour for our protection and deliverance. It will be an honour for me and on behalf of my citizens to drink with you and toast the future success of your long quest.'

He pressed a bell on his desk, summoning in a young clerk who had been clearly waiting with a tray with six glasses and a decanter of red wine with a plate of *langues de chat.* The wine was poured and another emotive and rather longer speech from the mayor took place, which ended in the final toast and the raising of glasses.

Olive, in her quiet voice, thanked the mayor. 'I have never visited this part of France before. It was too difficult for me to see the site where Ben must have died. Thank you, Monsieur Le Maire, for your kindness, understanding and your welcome to me, my daughter-in-law Pam and my friends. Also to you both, Messieurs Capliez and Colpart, for your interest and invaluable assistance. You have both been so very helpful to me.'

They left *la mairie* and Olive stepped into Frank's car, which followed the Frenchmen. It was only a matter of some seven or eight kilometres before they arrived in the small town of Iwuy, which was, nevertheless, larger than Rieux. Driving through the town with its shops, bars and a petrol garage, they came to a lane in the countryside where they stopped.

Ernest Capliez gathered them all and said it was now only some three hundred metres. Olive was pensive. She did not know how she would react after all these years. She would be seeing for the first time the exact place where Ben had met his death. She tried to visualise their last moments. They were crashing in flames. They must have known they had little or no chance of survival.

What were Ben's last thoughts? Was it a stark realisation

that life was going to leave him? Was he thinking of the enormous pain he might suffer in the fraction before death? Was he thinking of Kivi or the baby to come, whom he would never see and perhaps would be named Talia? Was he thinking of Olive and the life they had found together?

All these questions flitted momentarily across her mind as she stepped slowly and ponderously across the field with the others. And then she saw the crater. It wasn't quite as large as she had imagined. It was now fifty years ago and it might, she had thought, have filled in. But it was there. It was unmistakable. There it was, after fifty years – a clear indenture of some fifteen or even twenty square metres, just off from the centre of the large field. It was clearly identifiable, but grass had grown over it after all these years.

Here was the sacred ground, as Olive saw it, where Ben had breathed the last air into his lungs before the fatal crash. At least she had heard that the bodies had not been burned and had been recognisable, with their dog tags clearly marked with their identities. She assumed this must have been the same for Ben.

Frank and Kitty and the two Frenchmen waited at the edge of the indenture. They wanted to give Olive a moment to be on her own at this long-awaited meeting at Ben's place of death. Olive, now in the centre of the slight depression, looked at the ground for several minutes. She then knelt down at the epicentre of the crater and wept.

'Oh, Ben, I've missed you so much!' Her crying grew louder as she spoke to him as if he were living and present. 'Ben, you've missed your boys. They have missed you. They've grown to be such wonderful men with their own families. You would be very proud of them.

'Oh, Ben, if only you could rise and come back to me.'

She was in floods of tears and, as Kitty went to comfort her, Frank drew her back.

'Kitty, this is her moment of memory. Leave it for her. She has waited a very long time to be back with Ben. This is her homage to him. Give her the time and peace to be together with him.'

After several minutes, Olive rose to her feet. Now fully composed, she turned to Kitty. 'And now I have been to Ben, I want to go back to England. I may return shortly with a rabbi to say prayers over this sacred ground. But, before I do so, let us go to the cemetery at Iwuy to place a flower from the field on the grave of Sergeant Hutt and then on to the cemetery at Rieux to say a prayer over the graves of Ben's companions. Would you agree?'

'Of course, Olive,' Frank said. 'That is the best thing to do. It will be a privilege to take you and share in this memorable visit. But this must be very emotional for you. You're tired. After the cemetery at Rieux, we can leave for England. We can consider what more you might want to do back at home.'

At this, the six of them walked slowly away from the crater to their cars. Olive thanked each of them – M Capliez and M Colpart – and shook their hands most warmly, and they in turn, in the Gallic manner, planted kisses on her two cheeks.

Hands were shaken with Pam and the Humphries and once in their cars, they drove their separate ways.

18

January 1996

In January 1996, just seven months later, the *Cambrai Historical Magazine* published an article under the byline of Ernest Capliez and Cyriaque Colpart. It was headed: In Memory of Benjamin Bloom, British Airman Killed at Iwuy 16 June 1944.

The article read:

> 'By daybreak the German police are there. Very quickly five bodies are recovered and identified. The Germans take them to Rieux and they are buried in a communal grave alongside the seven comrades from the other aircraft.
>
> 'Some days later some children find the body of Sergeant Hutt in a cornfield and he is buried in the cemetery at Iwuy. But the body of Sergeant Bloom is missing.'

This article was pointed out to Marcel Lanes, who was eight years old at the time the plane came down in Iwuy. He read it carefully and then decided to approach the publishers. What he told them was awe-inspiring. They took a statement from him, which Marcel, now nearing his sixtieth birthday, carefully read and signed. He was told the Mayor of Rieux would like to meet him. Within two days, he was warmly received in the *mairie* and invited to drink coffee with the mayor and the two writers of the article.

'Monsieur Lanes, I have read your statement with great interest. Please give me your personal account of what you saw and heard on that early morning of the 16th of June 1944.'

'Well, Monsieur Le Maire, as you know, the plane came down and crashed in the field of Monsieur Dagniaux very early in the morning. It must have been around 1.30, although I couldn't swear to the exact time. It certainly woke us all up.

'It wasn't more than three hundred metres from us. I could see the flames from my window. Some people, including my dad, went out to see if they could rescue any survivors, but I heard next morning from my dad that there weren't any. They daren't touch the bodies since the German police would be coming and there would be hell to pay if they found we had interfered with the crash site.

'Next morning, I was up at my usual time of six o'clock. I would be at school for seven and back home for lunch at twelve. After that, I would work on the farm for the afternoon. This was quite normal, particularly in the summer months. In the agricultural communities, the children's help in the fields was expected and there was no school in the afternoons.

'But, as I went to leave for school just after six, I saw the Germans arrive in a lorry and a car. They were armed with rifles and some with automatic weapons. They were wearing their usual dove-grey uniforms. I saw one officer, who was in the car with a driver. He wore a black uniform with jackboots. I assumed he was SS as this was their usual uniform. Being curious, I went over to look and listen but was told to keep away from the wreckage.

'They laid out the bodies in a line and I counted them.

There were six. No question, I counted them carefully and recounted them as I knew my father would want to know. There was some consternation, and I caught the drift that they were missing one body – presumably there were seven in a crew. They began to take off the tags from around the necks of the corpses but one of them wore a necklace, a silver thread with the Jewish emblem, the Star of David.

'This was pointed out to the officer, who came to look. He checked the necklace and shouted, '*Ein gefluchtige Jude*!' which I understood later meant, if you will excuse the language, Monsieur Le Maire, 'a fucking Jew'. The officer barked a short command to his men to bury the body with the necklace in the ditch close to the hedge some two hundred metres away.

'Two of them carried the body and another two dug a grave with their shovels, and I saw no more. Later, perhaps a few days later, I saw the area where they had buried the airman, but I could not see exactly where as the ground had been levelled back and twigs and roughage had been strewn along the hedge line. It was at the time the British were launching an offensive against two crack Panzer divisions from the area between Caen and Bayeux. I thought the British would be with us within a week or so.

'I didn't mention what I had seen to my father as I didn't want him to get into trouble with the Germans so late in the war. So, Monsieur Le Maire, I kept my mouth closed until I read the article by these gentlemen. I thought it safe now to tell this story.'

Just short of six months after her visit to Iwuy, Olive received a letter from the Mayor of Rieux addressed in an embossed envelope with the crest of the town of Rieux.

'Dear Madame Bell,
It is with much joy and great relief that I am today able to give you some positive news of the late Sergeant Ben Bloom. You will recall when you were here that Messieurs Ernest Capliez and Cyriaque Colpart were to publish the story of the events of that fateful night of the 15th and 16th of June 1944 in the Cambrai Historical Magazine. *I enclose a copy of that publication. Some weeks after the issue, Monsieur Lanes came to see me. I attach a copy of his statement from which you will see that he witnessed Sergeant Bloom's body being buried in a ditch. This ditch has been recently excavated and the remains of a body were found. The one item that could show beyond doubt that it was the body of Sergeant Ben Bloom was the silver necklace with the Jewish emblem of the Shield of David found with his remains. The relic was reburied last Tuesday in the communal grave at Rieux with solemnity within twenty-four hours of his being found, so joining his comrades. I was present with the Mayor of Iwuy together with other dignitaries at the reburial. I was able to say a few words of thanksgiving for the late Sergeant Bloom.*

If you were to re-visit us, I shall advise our colleagues in Iwuy so that you can be assured of our every co-operation as to what you may wish to achieve.

With my felicitations

Jean Mayeux
La mairie, *Rieux'*

Olive clutched the letter and wept. 'Ben, after all this time, we have found you. You are at home now. You are at rest. I'm coming to see you.'

Pam comforted her and wept with her. It had been a journey of over fifty years. Olive briefly reflected on those years: years of hardship, of hopelessness at times but of never giving up.

'The boys must be told,' Olive told Pam.

'Of course. I shall tell Paul this evening. He will be so thrilled for you. I don't suppose Kivi will have any real memories. But at least Ben had been with him for a short time.'

'Pam, can you help me to trace Ben's brother and sisters? Some may still be alive, or at least their offspring. This will be a great opportunity to seal the reunion of the family. What better could we do than to invite them to such a ceremony to give respect and finality to Ben?'

Pam was playing with her glove, trying to place it in her handbag to join the other glove already there. She turned to her mother-in-law. 'Yes, of course. I think we're pretty good now at tracing family history! It'll be a pleasure, and let's hope we'll have results.'

'It'll not be easy after all this time. His brother, Bob, and his sisters may not still be alive, but certainly their offspring should be. It would be absolutely right to have them over here. Ben would have appreciated it as a proper place for a reconciliation.'

19

27 May 1999

Pam got to work as soon as she returned back home. She made every effort to trace Ben's siblings and their children. She had little to go on. No contacts with that family, no addresses and no one who might know of them. She telephoned many 'Blooms' in the London directory and explained to each of the listeners the reasons why she was calling. She was, she said, looking for Ben's brother, Bob, not even knowing whether he was alive. She had no idea of the surnames of Ben's sisters, who she presumed would now have married names. Pam had, however, always mentioned them in the hope she could be led to a contact who might have known their family story. She talked of them whenever she could speak with an interested person on the phone.

She found that many were fascinated by the family story, but no one she came across had had any connection apparently with Ben's family. She referred to the shoe factory in Hackney, which she found had been redeveloped into a block of flats some years earlier.

She had no joy either with the Royal Air Force, having written to the commanding officer of RAF Waterbeach who had no knowledge of Mrs Bloom, Ben's mother. Following the adjutant's advice in his written reply, she wrote to RAF Innsworth Gloucester, but they could not give any help. It appeared from her contacts with the National Pension Offices that Ben's mother had died in the early seventies and no one had been further entitled to pension rights.

Pam contacted the BBC through the introduction of a

friend, and they agreed to broadcast a message for anyone who could put them in touch with relatives of the late Sergeant Ben Bloom, who had died in his Lancaster Bomber in France in June 1944. But despite all Pam's efforts with many organisations and publications, she drew no result.

Finally, two years later, in 1998, Pam found two of Ben's sisters, having written to them – in their maiden names – through the Office of National Statistics, which had forwarded the letters on to them.

The sisters, now in their eighties, were in care, but fortunately neither were senile, although they were immobile. Pam was able to contact and meet with them. They were astonished to hear her story. They had known of Ben's missing in action from their mother and had presumed he had been killed when he had not returned after the war. They had also known of Olive and Ben's two boys but had not contacted her on the instructions of their mother, who ruled the family. They told Pam that they had much regretted this and had wanted to see the children who, after all, were nephews. They also had wanted to meet Olive and were not overly fussed she was not Jewish.

Through them, the detail of the news and the letters were eventually passed on to Ben's brother, Bob, who had been serving in a destroyer abroad when Ben had been killed.

Pam arranged for Olive to meet the two sisters in their care home. Notwithstanding the problems with their mother back in 1944, the meeting was a joyous occasion, and the ice broke immediately once they had been introduced to each other. Lily, now in her eighties, wrinkled and lined and sitting in a tall-backed armchair, told Pam, 'Mother had told us about Olive and the two children. My mother had never been easy and we all – that is, Bob and my sisters – were ashamed of what she had tried to do. We hadn't known about it till much later. We never knew where Olive lived, so we were never able to get in touch.

'I'm so pleased that Ben and Olive had a good life together, however short. I've never met the boys. Now each have their own family and, through you and Olive, Ben lives on. You know, they might like to contact Bob. He should be told. He lives in Bournemouth now.'

Pam contacted him, and he was amazed and overjoyed to hear the news of Ben's grave. He had realised Ben had been in love and had been caught by the anger of the gods, who should have been there to protect and help them both. He could not hide his joy and pleasure in knowing Ben had had a family and had enjoyed a life with Olive.

The sisters were insufficiently mobile for a journey to Rieux, but Bob was delighted to be invited.

Olive suggested the ceremony should be on Ben's seventy-eighth birthday, 27 May 1999 – fifty-five years after his death. Pam would make arrangements for their travel with the Humphreys and stay for two nights so as not to add to the strain of the occasion.

It was late in February 1999 when Olive received a phone call.

'Mrs Bell?' enquired the caller in a hesitant voice, clearly not absolutely certain that he was speaking to the right person.

'Yes, that's me. Who am I speaking to?'

'Mrs Bell, I am Reverend Leslie Hardman, the Jewish honorary chaplain to Her Majesty's Forces. I have just received a letter from Rabbi Eli Dahan of Lille, referring to the late Sergeant Benjamin Bloom, who lost his life on a bombing raid on the 16th of June 1944. I understand you were his consort and had two sons by him. Rabbi Dahan has outlined the full story of your amazing search for his body following his death in 1944.

'I understand you are arranging a "stone-setting" for Sergeant Bloom May next. I should be honoured and very much like to be present in my capacity of honorary chaplain to Her Majesty's Forces to give a Jewish remembrance with *Kaddish* to Ben. Would this be agreeable to you?'

Olive was taken aback at first. She hadn't realised this simple memorial service would reach the attention of the Jewish chaplain to the forces.

'Of course, Reverend Hardman. I am flattered you telephoned and honoured you would like to be present. May I take it that Rabbi Dahan will also be present? Can I ask you to liaise with him? I wouldn't wish to see him upset or removed from the service next May.'

'Yes, of course. I shall remain in touch with him and, if it is all right with you, I shall send him a suggested programme for the service and he and I can agree on who says what. We won't agree anything without your knowledge and consent. May I take your address so I can send you the programme for your approval before I send it on to the mayor?'

Olive gave her address. 'Well, I'm most grateful to you, Reverend Hardman. Ben would have appreciated your involvement and interest. It's really kind of you to take this on and come across to Rieux.'

'Not at all, Mrs Bell. From what I have heard of you both, you deserve everything we can offer.'

'Reverend Hardman, I hope you know that, although Ben came from a traditional Jewish family, I am Catholic. I know you will understand when I say I'm a "chained" woman. I was never able to obtain a divorce through my church. Ben and I could never marry, although we both wanted to. Although Ben wanted me to convert to Judaism for the children, I didn't feel I could desert the religion I was brought up as. But this did not spoil our wonderful relationship. I would not wish to disguise anything from you, Reverend.'

'Mrs Bell, I assure you I am well acquainted with the facts in your case. I want to be present because Ben died in the service of his country in war action. He deserves a Jewish burial and remembrance, which Rabbi Dahan and I will be able to give to him. I also have every admiration for you and your family for taking these steps to find Ben and to give to him and his family a form of peace and remembrance.

'There is just one more point, Mrs Bell. Because of Ben's celebrity and the manner of his being found after all these years, the Association of Jewish Ex-Servicemen and Women – Ajex – want to support the remembrance service too. I understand perhaps six or seven people want to come to Rieux. They will be wearing uniform suitable for ex-servicemen, dark blue blazers, berets, long white gauntlet gloves and with their standards. They will arrive in a minibus.

'They know, of course, how to form up in military fashion and when to raise and lower their standards. It will add a relevant military edge to the remembrance. The national chairman of Ajex is Gabriel Kaufman, whom I know very well. If you agree, I shall tell him and place him on the list of invitees.'

Olive did not have to think long. 'Reverend Hardman,' she said, 'Ben was always proud to be Jewish and I was proud of him that he was Jewish. It will be a blessing if Mr Kaufman and his party were to join us at the ceremony. I'll have to leave it to you to liaise with Rabbi Dahan and the mayor. I would also like to have a draft of the order of service so I'll know and can approve of everything that will happen.

'I never thought that a simple thanksgiving would become such a really meaningful service for Ben. I'm truly grateful to you, to the mayor and to Rabbi Dahan.'

It didn't take long for the Reverend Hardman and Rabbi Eli Dahan to agree the order of service. The draft programme was in English, Hebrew and French and headed with the bold lettering of Ajex. Olive and Pam carefully read it through and added 'The Laying of Wreaths.' Subsequently, Ajex added 'Sounding of the Last Post' followed by silence and then the reveille.

All was now set for 27 May. Lawrence Bloom, a distant cousin, rallied friends and extended members of the family, and a number came over the night before and stayed at the nearby hotel, the Chateau de la Motte Fenelon. It was the evening of the European Cup Final between Manchester United and Bayern Munich. It didn't help Lawrence or his companions that the televisions in their rooms were not properly functioning, so they missed the match. The omens, however, on the morning of the ceremony were good when the proprietor told them that Manchester United had won, both their goals coming in injury time.

It was a perfect late spring morning. It was a dry day, and the sun was shining, although one could not say it was hot, merely warm. The trees were in blossom and the fields were looking productive as Lawrence and his partners made their way by car to the cemetery in Rieux. It was not difficult to find.

Flags flew, and bunting was hanging from every conceivable area. The police, in smart uniforms with their long white gauntlets, were in line, and a number of French military officers and soldiers in their uniforms and kepis gave the occasion a military and dignified splendour.

A French military band was playing martial music when Olive, with Bob at her side and escorted by the two mayors, entered the cemetery and stood at the head of the crowd. She was wearing a Wedgewood-blue dress and a large, white-brimmed hat. She looked as she was – a dignified woman of considerable charm.

The Ajex members stood at attention close to the memorial stone for Ben and his late companions. In their dark blue blazers and berets with their long white gauntlets, they held their tall banners aloft, adding greatly to the solemnity and purpose of the gathering.

The service began with Rabbi Dahan reciting Psalm One in Hebrew, followed by Reverend Hardman reading in English the exhortation:

'Who may ascend the mountain of the Lord?
And who may stand in his holy place?
He that hath clean hands and a pure heart.
He shall receive a blessing from the Lord,
And righteousness from God of his salvation.'

This was followed by the reading of Psalm XVI in Hebrew and of Psalm XXIII in English.

The Mayor of Rieux then gave the formal address. He spoke first in French and his aide, a tall, young French lady, followed with the English translation.

'Mrs Bell, English friends, on behalf of both myself, the municipality of Rieux-en-Cambresis and my colleague, the mayor of our neighbouring municipality, Iwuy, I would like to say how touched we are at this moving story so tragically interrupted by war more than fifty years ago.

'Your presence here, Mrs Bell, your determination to find the remains of your fiancé who disappeared, demonstrate, in the image of the rose which has been planted, the eternity of your love for the late Sergeant Ben Bloom.

'For you and for our British neighbours, I will reiterate my gratitude, for you who in 1914–1918 and again in 1939–1945 were our allies to conquer the enemy. The military cemetery for those lost in 1914–1918 bears witness to this.

'Together with the men of my generation, I myself the son of a prisoner of war, I am still aware of the sacrifice made by Sergeant Bloom and the numerous British servicemen who contributed to our deliverance from the Nazis and their atrocities.

'To yourself and to Monsieur Le Rabbi and the Reverend Hardman, I must again voice our horror and disgust at the massacres which made victims of Jewish men and women. We will never relinquish the fight for the dignity and freedom of the soldiers of the last war. Thank you.'

After a short pause, loud applause from everyone except those on formal parade broke out and carried on for more than a minute, which to those present was a long time and well deserved. The mayor had caught the mood of the many witnesses in that cemetery on that May morning perfectly.

Reverend Hardman followed with a short address, which was personal to Olive and the Bloom family who were present.

He then proceeded in Hebrew, with the traditional memorial prayer for Ben which was followed by Kaddish led by Bob Bloom in Hebrew. The Ajex members laid the wreaths with great solemnity, and the Ajex bugler sounded the Last Post followed by the traditional silence. The quiet peace was broken by the bright and loud notes of the reveille.

The final hymn of 'Adon Alom' was sung with much gusto in Hebrew by the many members of the Jewish faith present.

Finally, the two mayors escorted Olive and the other members of the official party and guests to the *vin d'honneur* in the town hall.

Epilogue

13 September 2000

'Pam, there's one last task I want to achieve before I leave this world,' Olive announced.

'And what would that be?'

'Now we've found Ben and laid him to rest, a blessing to our union from His Holiness the pope,' Olive said, without any fear of contradiction at this lofty suggestion.

Pam paused momentarily to allow herself to consider whether Olive was serious. However, recovering quickly, she realised that, if Olive made a suggestion, it was wholly and unquestionably serious.

'Olive, on this occasion, you may be asking for the impossible! First, Ben was never Catholic. To gain an audience with the pope is well-nigh impossible. He isn't exactly waiting for the likes of you. I wouldn't know how to go about it. I suppose we should have to approach Father Anthony and see what he has to say on this subject.'

'Pam, we must do what we have to do. I want a blessing on our union from the pope. I haven't kept my faith for all these years, holding out against every effort to change it, for nothing. The pope may well accept my request for an audience. I'm eighty-four, Pam. I may not have long on this earth, and I want to try to obtain a papal blessing. It will be a fitting end to our lives, and Ben received *his* blessing in Rieux.'

'Fine, Olive. If that's what you want, let's see what can be done. Personally, I wouldn't give it a cat's chance in hell for success.'

Two days later, Pam met with Father Anthony in his office at the Church of the Trinity. She outlined the story of Olive, her convent upbringing, her staunch loyalty to her faith and referred to the finding of Ben's remains in 1996 and the services for Ben in Rieux. She explained that Olive was eighty-four years old and her wish was to have an audience with His Holiness in the Vatican and have her union with Ben blessed by him.

Father Anthony listened carefully to their story. He held his palms together and touched the top of his fingers with each hand, a sure sign of difficulty.

'It's never easy to obtain an audience with His Holiness. His time is taken up with so many matters of the church worldwide. There are so many people who want to meet with him. There are lists and lists of good and worthy people, all of whom have good reasons to offer as to why His Holiness should see them. I cannot see Olive being given such an opportunity.

'However, I would be happy to start the process. I will have to take a detailed statement from Olive. If I can recommend Olive further, I will submit my paper to the bishop's office, who will spend time considering the matter. If they were to further recommend such a request, the papers will be forwarded to the papal nuncio in London. If *he* were to accept the recommendation, he will forward the papers to the relevant office in the Vatican.

'There, it will be pored over by a committee, headed by a bishop, and the names for such an audience will be sifted. Eventually, and I could not put a timescale on any of this, it could be that an invitation to a public audience with His Holiness might be proffered. This would not, of course, be a private audience, but at the very best one limited to several hundred people, all of whom would have gone through this process from whatever country they come from.

'There will be no opportunity for Olive to meet the pontiff personally. It is always possible that as the pontiff moves along the lines of the faithful he would stop and say a few words to Olive, but I have to say, Pam, the chance of all this happening is remote. I shouldn't wish to give false hopes.'

'Well, this is not really encouraging, Father, but thank you for your forthright advice. I'll tell Olive everything you have said and go from there.'

Later in the cottage, after telling Olive what had occurred, Pam said, 'I find myself frustrated, irritated and nonplussed with the negativity surrounding this. It's not Father Anthony's fault. He was just pointing out the problems that lay ahead. If we were to follow his line of thought, we'll still be talking about this in ten years' time. I know what I'm going to do,' she said, with a note of finality. 'I'm going to call the Vatican!'

'Now you're talking, Pam! That's what I want to hear – action stations. Let's treat this as a mission. That's just what Ben would have said.'

Pam got busy. She found the number for the Vatican on Google and dialled. When the call was answered, Pam spoke first to ensure English would be spoken.

'Is that the office of the Vatican? May I speak to an English-speaking Bishop in respect of requests for an audience with His Holiness.'

The reply came from a man's voice in Italian English. 'Madam, may I have your name, telephone number and address in your country, *prego*?'

Pam gave this information, speaking with deliberate

slowness so the receiver could take down the detail. In fact, it was being recorded.

'Madam, I can put you through to a Bishop John. He is English and is much involved with applications for audiences with His Holiness. Please hold this line.'

Pam held on for some three minutes, which to her was a very long time. She thought she would never hear another voice and was beginning to think she should redial the number when a voice speaking in cultured, grave English asked, 'Madam Pam Bell, I believe. I am Bishop John. What can I do for you?'

Pam briefly outlined her request, which was met with the routine response that she must go through the well-worn traditional Catholic procedures of her parish priest before he could consider whether he could make a recommendation to his committee which dealt with papal audiences.

Pam asked his indulgence to relate Olive's story from her days in the convent to the finding of Ben's body. It took her just twenty minutes as she condensed the story and mentioned Ben's stone-setting ceremony in 1999 – and the values that these ceremonies held not only for Olive, but also for the communities of Rieux and Iwuy. She also told how Olive had always retained her Catholic faith, despite the pressures on her to change and convert.

'Bishop John, Olive is now eighty-four years old and her wish before she passes on is to have received the support and blessing from His Holiness for her union with Ben.

'If she is required to go through the procedures of her parish priest, his bishop and papal nuncio before they reach you in the Vatican, she is unlikely to survive the time it will take. Olive is frail at present but has the energy and capability to travel to Rome and to pay her respects and devotion to

His Holiness. It will be a blessing to her and the late Benjamin Bloom if you could allow her to be included in an audience.'

Bishop John had listened without interruption to Pam's related history of the relationship between Ben and Olive – the two soulmates from two different religions.

'Mrs Bell, or Pam, if I may, your story of Olive and Ben is remarkable and most interesting. It is unique, in my experience. I want you to write to me, putting everything you have told me in as much detail as you can, from Olive's time in the convent until the current period, giving dates, her life and history with Ben. Send it for my personal attention at the Vatican.

'I give you my consent not to proceed through your priest. As soon as I can verify what you have told me, I shall send to Olive and to you as her consort an invitation to an audience with His Holiness. It will not be possible to arrange a private audience, but I am certain His Holiness will refer to Olive in his message delivered on that day.

'May the blessings of the Lord be upon you – and Olive.'

Pam could hardly take in what she had just heard. She immediately made a detailed note of the conversation in her 'Olive' booklet, which contained all the correspondence with the mayors of Rieux and Iwuy, in case she woke up later and thought it had been a dream.

And so later that year, on 13 September 2000, Olive, accompanied by Pam, presented her embossed Vatican invitation to the Catholic Officer of the Guard in his formal ancient uniform and plumed helmet at the entrance to the Aula Paolo V1 (the Pope Paul V1 Audience Hall) within the Vatican.

They were admitted and escorted to their seats in the

front row. As they sat waiting for His Holiness Pope John Paul the Second to arrive, a high clergyman dressed in formal clothes, an orange-coloured sash running from his right shoulder to his left hip and a coloured skull cap covering the crown of his head, stopped and turned along the front row. He looked at Olive and Pam and whispered, 'You must be Olive Bell,' and, looking at Pam, 'and you, Pam. I am Bishop John, John Harvey. I am so pleased you were able to be with us this morning.'

'Your Eminence, it is we who thank you. This invitation was divinely inspired to us! It's a dream I have had since I was a young woman in the convent in London to be here in God's House in the Vatican in the presence of his vicar, His Holiness, the pope. This is a blessing you have bestowed on us,' said Olive.

The bishop inclined his head in a slight bow. 'That is very gracious of you. I know you will both enjoy – and be satisfied by – this experience.' And he moved on his way towards the chairs at the side of the dais, which were now filling with high church dignitaries.

Olive cast her eyes around the ornate and gilded room with such a high ceiling. Pillars with gold cornices stood in dignified lines on each side of the audience chamber, reaching high to the heavens where the ceiling to the chamber must have been more than hundred and fifty feet. The long, tall, stained-glass windows, each only some twenty feet apart and which stretched down the length of the hall, throwing their colours on to the chamber floor in great shafts of light. Each window depicted an analogy from the Bible. There was a discreet low tone of quiet speaking as all who were there sat in awe of their surroundings with its historic values and architectural beauty.

Olive had to pinch herself thinking she was there in the Vatican and shortly to see and listen to the pope giving his monthly message.

And then, without any fanfare or announcement, a solemn short procession of guards in their Swiss papal uniforms escorted the short figure dressed all in white with a white skull cap on his head, supported behind him by a number of cardinals dressed in their black and dark crimson robes and crimson skull caps.

His Holiness came to the dais in the centre of the forefront, some ten metres from the front seats, and slightly raised by a few steps in the marble surround. All had risen when His Holiness entered the chamber. And now he paused. He looked round the chamber as if greeting each person individually with his well-known benign smile on his broad and expansive face and made a movement with his hands to signify all should now sit.

He sat in a high-backed comfortable-looking armchair between two cardinals sitting on more austere chairs, facing the audience. The attending cardinals and bishops sat in four lines of chairs to the pope's left, facing him. Behind the pontiff, stood the huge magnificent sculpture by Pericle Fazzini of La Resurrezione.

The pope first spoke in Italian and then changed to German and finally to English. Olive felt His Holiness was looking directly at her, sitting, as she was, in the front row.

Wide-eyed and in shock, she heard His Holiness say the words she would never ever forget.

'And I bless the union, after so many years of searching for the truth, which was finally found in the sacred earth of the fields in northern France, of the souls of Benjamin Bloom and Olive Bell.'

20088179R00139

Printed in Great Britain
by Amazon